CALEB'S CROSS

A TWISTY CHRISTIAN MYSTERY NOVEL

URCELIA TEIXEIRA

CALEB'S CROSS

A TWISTY CHRISTIAN MYSTERY NOVEL

ANGUS REID MYSTERIES - BOOK I I I

URCELIA TEIXEIRA

AWARD WINNING AUTHOR

CALEB'S CROSS

A TWISTY CHRISTIAN MYSTERY NOVEL

ANGUS REID MYSTERIES BOOK III

URCELIA TEIXEIRA

E-book © ISBN: 978-0-639-84346-9

Paperback © ISBN: 978-0-6398434-9-0

Large Print Paperback © ISBN: 978-1-928537-75-5

Published by Purpose Bound Press Written by Urcelia Teixeira

First edition

Urcelia Teixeira

Wiltshire, UK

https://www.urcelia.com

START WITH ...

BOOK 1 IN THE ANGUS REID MYSTERIES SERIES

A MISSING TEEN. A TOWN BURIED IN SECRETS. A MOTHER WHO WOULD DO ANYTHING TO SAVE HER SON.

Get it here now

books.urcelia.com/jacobswell

INSPIRED BY

They have also healed the hurt of My people slightly,
Saying,
'Peace, peace!' When *there is* no peace.

Jeremiah 6:14
(NKJV)

PREFACE

He could run and hide, pretend like everyone else.
Only there isn't a corner secret enough that would bury
the turmoil brewing within.
For within the depths of his soul, the crossroads between
heaven and hell lie festering.

Until light punctures the shadows and it all comes
crashing down...

CHAPTER ONE

Rachel stared at the lifeless body that lay in a lump at her feet. She was going to hell, one way or the other, and she didn't need the *Ordnung* to confirm it. She should be afraid, have remorse, or even the smallest measure of pity for seeing him like this, dead on the floor.

Except, she didn't. She was glad he was dead.

That thought alone was enough to land her in the fiery furnace. Yet, in that moment, the idea of not entering heaven didn't scare her. She had already decided that the netherworld couldn't possibly be worse than the purgatory she'd been living here on earth. At least since the first time she came to see the doctor. A fate she could not escape. For what the elders said to do, one never questioned.

She recalled the conversation she had overheard one Sunday after church.

"Perhaps the time has come for Rachel to see the

chiropractor," one elder had said to her father." To which another added, "She's your only daughter and it's your saintly obligation to make sure she's properly prepared for her holy calling."

Naturally, her parents accepted their council. Why would they not? When an elder advised, you obeyed.

The others told her it was what was required once a young woman neared the age of courting. Everyone she knew had seen the doctor at some stage, especially before they could be married and have children. She couldn't stop it even if she wanted to. It was as the elder had said, preparation for her holy calling—which was to marry and raise children. A calling she never wanted. She wanted more. Not that she truly knew what else there was waiting for her in the world of the English. But she had heard those who had come back from their *rumspringa* tell stories of the amazing things they had experienced in the English world. Things she now wanted more than ever.

Never this.

A flicker of sadness tugged at her heart. She did what was expected of her in obedience to her father. If only her father knew what these visits to the doctor were really about. That the *good doctor*'s so-called chiropractic adjustments had nothing to do with improving her posture or making sure her body could one day handle childbirth. That none of it felt right or holy. That he was creepy and made her feel strange. That he acted differently when her mother was in the room. If only they all knew. Perhaps they did and it was what was intended to happen during these visits. She would never know. These things were not spoken of. Gossiping would get her shunned.

She snickered at the thought of a shunning. None of that mattered now that the doctor was dead. She'd earned a far worse punishment than being shunned or even excommunicated.

For a moment, she just stood there, alone in the room staring at the man who had been haunting her thoughts. There will be no more *adjustments* made by him, she thought.

Grim satisfaction had seeped into her bones. Justice was served and in her solitary world of secrets, the line between salvation and despair grew more elusive by the moment.

Her eyes took in the strange way the doctor's body was curled up. He must have died a painful death, she thought when she saw the way his fingers were bent into claws.

A sudden chill ran down her spine. What if he wasn't dead? What if he was just practicing a strange adjustment on himself? What if her nightmare wasn't over?

She carefully shuffled a few steps closer to the body and lightly tapped the side of his leg with the black tip of her shoe. He didn't move. She waited, then kicked his leg again, this time harder before she quickly backed away from his body. Still nothing happened. She should run for the hills, but something made her stay. She had to be sure he was dead.

Like a wolf circling its prey, she slowly moved around his body, her eyes fixed on him, anticipating that he would move at any moment.

When she reached his head and saw his eyes, open wide and cold, her heart nearly stopped and she jumped backward, bumping into the cushiony table he'd always made her lay down on. A jumble of emotions pushed into her throat, filling her senses with guilt, shame, hatred, and fear all at once. The doctor's lifeless eyes remained fixed on hers, never wavering, never looking away. It was the most ghastly thing she had ever seen in her nearly sixteen years of life. But it was confirmation, nonetheless. He was for sure dead.

She studied his face more intently, the deep lines around his eyes and his long, white beard telling of his age. If she didn't know any better, he could have easily passed as one of the elders in their community, although she was grateful he wasn't. That would have made her life even more unbearable.

The room suddenly felt heavy with the weight of secrets; the air thickened by the sins that lingered in the stillness. She wondered how many others there had been before her. Or was it only her? The pale light from the flickering bulb overhead cast a morbid glow on the scene, revealing the stark reality of her predicament.

Her eyes darted around the room as if to make sure no one else was there. Or perhaps to make sure she left no trace behind. She wasn't sure. But what she did know was that she needed to get out of there before her mother came for her.

She bolted for the door, her heart pounding in her chest, a desperate rhythm that seemed to echo the sudden turmoil that had taken root in her soul.

Once outside the loft room, she ran down the partially concealed wooden stairs, pulling her royal blue dress up to her knees so she wouldn't miss a step and fall. When she finally reached the last few steps, she held back against the wall and snuck a peek at the elderly woman who normally sat behind the large wooden desk in the downstairs room.

Although the woman had always been very friendly with her, Rachel had no idea how she would explain her abrupt departure if she were seen running away so soon into her appointment. At least her hearing was not all that great. That was half the battle won and when Rachel saw that the woman's back was turned toward the exit, her heart filled with hope.

Seizing the moment, she tiptoed toward the exit, quietly inching her way to the door. She briefly looked back over her shoulder before she successfully escaped from the doctor's office.

CHAPTER TWO

Once outside, Rachel broke into a sprint and made a beeline for the horse and buggy where one of her older cousins had secured it to a large maple tree down the road. He sat reading his book in the shade of the tree when she came bolting toward him.

"That was quick," he said, slamming shut the book he was clearly not interested in. He moved over to make space for her to sit next to him under the tree.

"We need to go," Rachel replied in haste, ignoring his gesture. She was already halfway into the buggy when he answered back.

"I'd like nothing more, but our mothers are still across the road getting sewing supplies. And by the sounds of it they might be a while. Something to do with the quilt they're making for Jeremiah's wedding."

Rachel's startled look drew a frown from her cousin.

"Why, what's the hurry?" he probed.

Rachel nervously glanced back in the direction of the doctor's office then climbed out of the buggy before making a hasty turn toward the supply shop across the road.

"What's gotten into you, Rachel Beiler? You're acting like a cow in season," he yelled after her.

But she'd already crossed the road and burst into the small general supply shop.

The overhead chime announced her entry and she cringed at the sharp sound. Her eyes soon found her mother and aunt in the back of the small shop, and she rushed toward them.

"I'm done; we can go now," she blurted out when her mother cast a surprised glance her way.

"Already?"

Rachel gave a furious nod as she spoke, "Uh-huh, and the doctor says I don't need to come back for any more treatments."

It was a lie, she knew. The first one she'd ever told her mother. Another reason her soul would land in the inferno for an eternity.

Her aunt's lips pulled into a proud grin.

"Well then, Lydia, it looks like you might be giving your only daughter's hand in marriage sooner than we thought."

Lydia clicked her tongue.

"Don't be so quick with your words, Mariah. My daughter is far too young to get married."

"The elders didn't seem to think so, and who are we to argue," Mariah said, her words ending with a mischievous wink before she turned and smiled at Rachel.

Rachel's stomach turned. If only they knew.

RACHEL SAT QUIETLY in the back of the buggy, her mind preoccupied with whether she'd managed to get away with her lie and what it would do to her family if word ever got out. It wouldn't be long before someone found the doctor in his office. What if they connected the dots and came for her?

She wedged two fingers behind the collar of her dress, tugging at the white starched fabric that now cut into her throat.

"Is everything all right, Rachel?" her mother asked. "You look a bit too pale for my liking."

Rachel nodded and followed her lie with a forced smile. Was it lying when you didn't say the words out loud? she wondered, then quickly looked away at the passing fields. She tried to focus on the patches of snow that had come early, but all she wanted to do was get back to her chores and the safe confines of the community. Tending to the animals always calmed her down.

Her conscience nagged at her. She should tell her mother,

confess the whole thing. It was the right thing to do. Perhaps she could while they were working on Jeremiah's new quilt, when her mother was always her happiest. But as soon as the thought came, she shrugged it off. Telling her mother would bring nothing but shame on the family. Her father would have to go before the council and who knows what they would decide. A sin this big would surely have them all excommunicated. No, she couldn't risk it, couldn't do it to them. It would be better if she were the only one to face perdition.

She contemplated her fate, her heart heavy as reality sank in. If only Caleb was around to tell her what to do. He'd know. He was wise like that. He had already faced the council's judgement.

As their mother's only children, it had always only been the two of them. Even though he was ten years older than her, he never treated her like a child. Sadness tugged at her heart. She missed her brother. It had been so long since she last saw him at the bridge, when they got caught and she spent fourteen days in shunning. Why did Caleb have to leave? Why couldn't he just join the church, get baptized, and live out his life with their family, with her?

She recalled their last secret meeting at the bridge. He had said that living among the English was far better than living with the Amish. That there was a whole world to be seen and explored. A world with fewer rules. But if you asked her, the real reason he chose not to come back to the community after his *rumspringa* was that he didn't want to be a farmer like their father. And as the only son, it would have been decided for him. Caleb was too smart to be a farmer. He liked working with numbers too much and he was so good when it came to discussing different points of view. It was like he possessed a gift to see beyond what was taught in the *Ordnung*. That gift had landed him in trouble too many times to count. For as long as she could remember, he challenged the rules and said they didn't make sense. And it only got worse after his *rumspringa*.

A faint smile settled on her young face. At least they had their letters. She couldn't survive without them. And if she'd managed to keep the letters between them a secret, she could keep anything a secret. Unless the vet in Weyport told on them. Caleb had somehow persuaded him to sneak their letters in and out whenever he was needed to enter their community to tend to a colicky horse. If it were not for him, she would never have been able to stay in touch with her brother. Even though she had heard that Weyport was only forty minutes away, no one ever traveled that far away from the Amish community.

The excitement of thinking about the letters brought with it a glimmer of hope when she recalled that the vet was due to come around the next day. She had forgotten all about it. She nearly squealed aloud when she realized that there could be another letter from Caleb. She would use tonight to write him another letter and ask if he could meet her at the bridge one more time. She had to tell him her side, explain why she did what she did. And if it was the last letter she ever got to write him or the last time she'd see him it would be enough for her.

The horse noisily flapped his lips as soon as her cousin turned their buggy off the road and drove over the Amish property lines. Relief finally banished the knots in her stomach. In time the guilt and shame would dissipate too, she was certain. At funerals, Bishop Jedediah always said that time brings about healing and that one's spirit finds peace in the small blessings of life. She'd heal too, and no one but Caleb would ever know her secret. And perhaps one day, when she arrived at the heavenly gates and pleaded her case, God will understand and grant her His grace to enter into heaven.

CHAPTER THREE

Rachel stood at the edge of the meticulously tended fields at the top of the small embankment, her simple bright blue dress rustling in the chilly evening breeze as the sun dipped below the horizon. Between the dense trees on the other side of the stream that rushed below, the sun had turned the sky an inviting orangey-pink color. Threatening clouds smothered the amber skies, hinting that they were in for a cold night and she mindlessly pulled her sleeves lower over her cold hands as she took it all in. The wooden fence, weathered by time, marked the boundary of the only world she had ever known—a world where faith, innocence, and simplicity were meant to be what set them apart from what lay on the other side. But she had on many occasions pondered if the boundaries were intended to keep them from escaping instead. Or perhaps it spoke of protection from the evil she already knew lurked outside the safe compounds of their community. Either way it was a boundary they were forbidden to cross and for the most part, she honored that unwritten law. Except for days like today.

Without any further thought, she crouched down and squeezed her body through the gap between the wooden crossbars of the fence, glancing over her shoulder to make sure no one was around. She knew the chances of being caught were slim—no one ever came to the far edges of the community. Also, this wasn't the first time she stepped outside the boundary. It was where she came to clear her head and to cry. This time she needed to be quick; it was nearly time to help her mother with the evening supper and tardiness would earn her a harsh reprimand. Not to mention that her mother would send her cousins to come looking for her.

Careful not to slide down the small slope where the icy leaves made the ground unsteady beneath her shoes, she inched her way down to the stream. Once during the summer, she had tried to wade her way to the other side, underestimated the depth and strength of the current, and nearly didn't make it back to dry land. Since then, she made sure she stayed well clear of the water. Besides, just being there, watching the frothy white water course over the rocks was all she needed anyway. The calm rushing of the water soothed her soul, and it was worth sneaking off between her chores to find solace in it. It was the only place she could be alone with her thoughts...and secrets.

Her eyes settled on a turbulent spot in the center of the rocky river. Disappointment had burrowed a hiding place deep inside her heart and she found her mood as dark and restless as the spot in the river. She had waited all day for the vet but for whatever the reason, he never came.

She slipped one hand into the pocket of her coat and folded it around the letter she had intended to sneak to Caleb. It took all the courage she could muster to share her heart with him, to share what happened every time she saw the doctor. And what happened the last time she was there. She very nearly didn't go through with it. But she wrote the letter nonetheless, needing desperately to clear her conscience.

Perhaps it was a blessing in disguise that the animal doctor hadn't come. Thinking about it now, she wasn't sure how Caleb would react to her letter if he were to read it. At first, she thought she'd save the letter for the next time the veterinarian came to visit and see if word about the chiropractor got out. But having thought about it all day, she was no longer sure she wanted to spill her heart. Her confession would bring nothing but shame and judgement on her and her family. But in truth, there was something far more pressing on her heart. She knew she would never be able to live if her only brother and best friend blamed and judged her for the part she played in everything. As the elders often said, guilt always had two sides.

She pulled the letter out and stared at the carefully crafted hand lettering she'd taken great care to perfect.

Her eyes lingered on the handmade paper she chose, admiring the beauty of the rose petals she had used when she made it herself a few weeks earlier. It would be a waste of her talents, but she decided to toss the letter in the wood burner when she and her mother prepared dinner. She crumpled up the stiff paper popping the wax seal away from the paper in the process and slipped the letter back inside her pocket. But when she pulled her hand out, the letter came as well and tumbled down her dress, dropping onto the ground next to her feet.

"Oh no!" She yelped and snatched after it but the crisp breeze had already scooped it up and deposited it into the water.

Dashing after it, Rachel nearly slipped on the icy leaves but caught her balance just in time. The crumpled letter got pushed farther from the river's edge to where it was quickly swept into the current. She watched as the scrunched up envelope caught on a clump of twigs and wet leaves before the fast-moving water unhooked it and took it downstream.

Rachel shrieked and ran after it along the rugged bank, careful not to slip and fall into the freezing water. But the ground was muddy and unsteady beneath her shoes. Before she could catch the letter that bopped between the rocks and disappearing beneath the frothy white water, her foot slipped and she plunged into the icy stream.

Instantly the cold water sent shockwaves through her body, briefly knocking her breath away. She pushed herself up, grabbing onto anything she could to pull her already numb body onto the embankment. The weight of her soaked coat made it much harder and before long, exhaustion got the better of her. Fear overwhelmed her senses and moments later the rushing water pulled her body deeper into the current. She felt her covering leave her head then glimpsed it floating past her. With numb fingers she grabbed onto a large boulder but the water ripped her away almost instantly, dragging her body farther away from safety. Something hard bumped up against her hip and tossed her around before the water pushed her head under. Rachel wanted to scream for help, but her body didn't react no matter how hard she tried. She had lost all sense of direction and was struggling to find which way was up. Icy water filled her lungs and her wide-stretched eyes felt as if they were frozen solid in her head. For the shortest of moments, air caressed her face as her head briefly bopped above the waterline. Gasping and spluttering for air, her arms flailed in search of something to grab onto, her body bouncing around in the white water. Too exhausted and cold to fight against the strong current, she yielded, focusing only on keeping her head above the water.

Until she felt the sharp rock slice into the back of her head and everything around her instantly went black.

CHAPTER FOUR

When the call came in on his cell phone, Angus was offloading the last of the boxes from the U-Haul trailer. Dumping the box of mismatched pots and pans on the kitchen floor, he scrambled for the phone he had buried in his back pocket.

"What's up?" he answered when he noticed that the call was coming from Tammy at the office.

"Sorry to interrupt your house move, Sheriff, but duty calls," Tammy started, her words tinged with humor before she switched to a more professional tone. "Miguel's still held up with the union dispute at the boatyard otherwise I wouldn't have bothered you until tomorrow."

"Crime never picks the right moment, right?" he joked back. "What's going on?"

"A 9-1-1 call just came in. A chiropractor, found dead

in his office a little ways outside of Weyport. His assistant came across him when she was closing up for the day. Said she found him in a horrific state—her words not mine. No idea what that means exactly. She was quite distraught to say the least. I have a patrol car on the way there already."

Angus shoved the box to one side with his foot and glanced at the time on his watch.

"To tell you the truth, Tammy, I was about to call it a day anyway. I can do with a break from the move. There's not much left to do today that can't wait until tomorrow."

"I'm patching the details through to you now, Sheriff. It's about forty minutes north from here, a small rural town that mostly serves the nearby Amish community. There's not much happening there so very few people know it even exists."

Angus snickered.

"There's not a day that goes by that this county doesn't surprise me with something new," he replied, already halfway through changing into his uniform when he added, "I'm assuming you've already sent the call through to Dr. Delaney."

"I'm actually doing that as we speak. She should arrive at the scene shortly after you. Forensics should also be on their way by now."

"And the patrol car? How far out are they?"

"The deputies should be on the scene in about fifteen minutes. I ran through the normal crime scene protocol with the caller so hopefully they'll get there before any evidence is contaminated. I told her to wait outside and not let anyone in, but word tends to get around pretty quickly in these little towns. I'll stay on top of it and wait until the car gets there before I knock off for the day."

"Sounds good and great work, Tammy," he added as he shut the door to his new home behind him.

THE SO-CALLED RURAL town was three streets and several buildings short of being able to claim the title and left Angus somewhat deflated when he arrived at the scene of the crime. His two deputies had already secured the perimeter and stood outside talking to an elderly woman, her tiny frame hunched over, her face as white as her neatly pinned-up hair.

Angus scanned up and down the short road when he got out of his car. Lined with four perfectly spaced large maple trees on both sides it was dead quiet. Across the street two Amish men stood with their arms crossed, watching from the porch of a general store that looked as if it had come straight off the set of a western movie. One of them tipped his head ever so gently in Angus' direction followed by the second man. Angus mimicked the greeting and took in the rest of the buildings that completed the one-horse settlement. There appeared to be a small clothing shop displaying nothing but two kinds of winter coats and a few pairs of black shoes in the window. The other buildings had no signage and were equally unassuming in appearance. Unlike what they'd ordinarily expect to see at a crime scene, there were no inquisitive minds hovering around. In fact, apart from the two Amish men in front of the store, there was no one anywhere in sight. It was as if whoever occupied the buildings was hiding intentionally—or had run away.

Angus turned his attention back to the simple looking house that bore a large wooden sign marking the doctor's chiropractic practice. He couldn't help but wonder if indeed a crime was committed or if the doctor might have succumbed to natural causes. There wasn't anything or anyone who seemed suspicious or even the slightest bit curious about their presence.

Before he had time to reflect on anything else, the elderly woman's hand waved him down and she stormed down the manicured garden path toward him, her voice surprisingly loud for such a small frame.

"Are you the sheriff? Come, come." She had him by the arm before Angus could answer. "He's in there, it's a horrific sight, Sheriff, come," she continued as she pushed and pulled him up the short path to the entrance, her small feet shuffling hastily across the tidy cobbled path.

She reached for the doorknob and was about to open the door for him when Angus stopped her, having to bend down to make eye contact. His voice was gentle and patient when he spoke.

"Ma'am, it's best you don't touch anything until we've done our forensic investigation. We don't want to spoil any evidence that might help us solve the case. I'm assuming you were the one who found him."

She nodded.

"I'm Sheriff Angus Reid." He paused, inviting her to introduce herself.

"Grace Walker," her voice was a near whisper.

"What was the nature of your relationship with the doctor?" He ushered her down the modest porch toward a small patch of roses.

She briefly glanced back at the house as if she didn't want to leave it behind then answered.

"He's my...was my employer. I've worked for him nearly thirty years." A soft whimper escaped before she continued. "I don't understand who would do such an evil thing, Sheriff. He's one of the kindest men I've ever known, gave his heart and soul to his work. Ask any of the Amish and they'll tell you how much he does...did for them. It's just horrific."

She covered her mouth with her fingertips.

"I'm deeply sorry for your loss, Ms. Walker. I hate to ask but could you tell me how you found him?"

She took a shallow breath before she answered.

"I always close up at the end of the day. Dr. Fisher usually leaves at four but today his last appointment was at two and he had said that he'd probably leave straight after. I didn't see or hear him leave, but then my hearing isn't what it used to be. I just assumed he walked her out and left when she did. That's why I went up to his office to make sure, before I locked up. But then I found him on the floor..." she squealed and buried her face in her small hands.

Her whimpers turned into a steady sob and Angus lifted his chin toward one of his deputies who stood close by.

"I'll do everything I can to find out what happened here, Ms. Walker. Deputy Allen will take good care of you while I look inside. We're going to need you to come in for a formal statement though. Will that be okay?"

"Tonight? I can't. I need to go home to my cats. If they don't eat on time it throws their tummies out, you know?"

Angus tried to conceal his amusement.

"Do you live nearby, Ms. Walker?"

She pointed to a house at the end of the short street.

"Just over there, you see, the one with the large maple out front."

"I'll send a car to fetch you in the morning if that's okay."

She nodded, tucking a stray hair back into the neat bun on her head.

"One more question then I'll let you go, Ms. Walker. Did anyone else work here besides you?"

She looked at him with annoyance, a slight frown between her nearly invisible white brows as she cocked her head to one side.

"No, of course not, it's only me. It's always only been me." Her voice broke as she whispered the words before the deputy led her away.

CHAPTER FIVE

Dr. Murphy Delaney's car pulled up in front of the crime scene moments before her forensics team arrived. When she got out and walked toward Angus, he saw the same look on her face that he must have had when he first took in the quiet little town.

"I know what you're thinking, Dr. Delaney. How could I hide this little gem from you, right?" He gave a mischievous smile and she smiled back.

"Ha, that's funny, Reid, but no, I was actually wondering why anyone would want to commit a murder in a place that seems so at peace."

"If indeed it is a homicide. I've not been inside yet but I find it hard to imagine."

"You don't think we have a homicide on our hands? And why's that?" Murphy questioned as she tied back her hair and pulled on a pair of latex gloves.

"Let's just say I'm not yet convinced. So far, there's nothing that tells me otherwise. No sign of any breaking and entering; no suspects looming around; no people period. Just his assistant who found him dead on the floor in his office. And she says she's been here all day. But I've been wrong before so I guess we're about to find out, aren't we? I mean, that's why you're here. You're the ME." He winked then added, "After you, Dr. Delaney."

Murphy ignored his playful charm and entered the house, pausing just inside the door, her eyes scanning through the large open area.

"Am I missing something? Where's the body?"

"I believe we will find our victim in his office upstairs. If only we knew where the stairs were."

"This way, Sheriff," one of his deputies said as he pointed out the perfectly obscured staircase.

"Interesting, I totally missed it from this angle," Angus said.

As he walked toward it, he briefly turned to one of the forensic specialists who stood nearby.

"Make sure you comb this place for evidence. If in fact there is a killer on the loose, it seems he walked in and out of here through the front door. Unless there's another entrance we haven't seen yet."

Angus paused at the bottom of the stairs before he turned to one of his deputies.

"Check if there are any windows or doors in the back. I've never had a case where the killer left through the front door in broad daylight. There has to be another way he could have slipped out without Ms. Walker seeing him."

The deputy acknowledged the directive and Angus followed Murphy up the stairs. When they stepped into Dr. Fisher's office, they paused in the doorway, each silently taking in the scene.

"Not a single thing is out of place in here," Murphy commented then walked over to where the body lay on the floor.

"Well," she said with surprise, "this isn't something I see every day."

Angus crossed the room to join her.

"His assistant was right. That *is* a horrific sight. I can see the horror even in his lifeless eyes. Heart attack perhaps?"

Murphy was on her knees next to the body.

"That's highly unlikely. Look at his hands. They're all curled up. This guy was in a lot of pain when he died and judging from his eyes, he went quickly."

The photographer gave the thumbs-up that he'd completed the first set of forensic photos and Murphy proceeded to inspect the body while he followed along.

"There's no blood, no sign of injury anywhere. If it weren't for the fact that there aren't any burn marks on his body, I would have guessed he was electrocuted. But I can safely rule that out too."

Angus changed position as he surveyed the body.

"So let me get this straight, Murphy. Are you telling

me this guy was not electrocuted, shot, stabbed, or had a heart attack?"

"It would appear so, yes, and it's not a drug overdose or epileptic fit either. Of course, a tox screen should tell us more, but at first glance, I see no evidence suggesting any of those as the COD."

Angus had his hands on his hips, frustration pouring from his body.

"I don't think I've ever seen such a clean crime scene. There's not a single drop of blood or sign of any struggle. I mean, his desk is pristine."

Murphy's attention was on the victim's neck.

"No evidence of puncture wounds either. I must admit, Angus, this one seems as strange a case as I've ever seen," she announced while inspecting each of the victim's hands.

"That makes two of us, Murphy." He paused then continued. "Okay, so let's just assume Dr. Fisher was murdered. I guess the next obvious question should be why? What motive would anyone in a one-horse ghost town like this have? And, apart from the assistant and the two Amish men observing from across the street, there isn't a single other person anywhere in sight. Why is that?"

"Now that'll be your job, Sheriff, but I will confirm that I am just as baffled by this one as you, and I don't say that easily. I've had my fair share of bodies on my table, and I've never seen severe rigor set in this quickly."

"What do you mean quickly? Look at his body, his

hands. This guy has been dead at least twelve hours," Angus said.

"Well, I'm sorry to tell you, but you're wrong on that one. Liver temp suggests otherwise. Our doctor has only been dead a few hours, four tops."

"That can't be right. His entire body is as stiff as a board."

"I bet you a prime steak at Floyd's that I'll find Dr. Fisher's lunch still entirely undigested in his stomach. He died recently and very quickly. And before you suggest he had an aneurysm, I can rule that one out too. There's no visible hemorrhaging either."

Murphy pushed herself off the floor, pulled off one of her latex gloves, and stuck out a hand to shake on the bet.

Angus gave a wide grin.

"You're that sure, Murphy."

She nodded, teasing him with a smile.

"Fine," Angus said shaking her hand, "but if I win, I'll cook you that steak at my house instead. Deal?"

"Deal." She slipped another glove back on her hand.

"How is everything going with the move anyway?" she asked as she turned her attention back to the body.

"I have a bit of unpacking ahead of me, but it felt good to finally empty my storage unit. It was like opening gifts on Christmas morning. I had forgotten about half the things I pulled out of storage. But I won't lie, it feels great to have a place to call home again."

"I bet. I'd say you got yourself one special little home

there, Angus. The Richardsons have lived in that house for as long as Weyport's been in existence and Patty was one great homemaker. I'm sure you're going to be very happy there."

"That's kind of you to say, Murphy, thanks. I do feel like I struck gold. I was beginning to think I'll never find a house in this town."

"It just shows you how everything works out exactly as it should, right? I mean, Patty and Daniel finally have the son they've always wanted and now they get a chance to get to know him. And who doesn't want to live in Nashville?"

"I don't," he winked. "I have everything I've always wanted right here in Weyport."

Murphy rolled her eyes playfully.

"Don't you have a murderer to catch, Sheriff?"

"I don't know, Doc, do I? You're sure this guy didn't die of natural causes."

The look in Murphy's eyes was as serious as the dead doctor on the floor beside her.

"I don't yet know what killed this guy, Angus, but I have no doubt in my mind that whatever it was, was not natural. Dr. Fisher was definitely murdered."

CHAPTER SIX

By the time Angus stepped outside, it was starting to get dark and the modest town looked even more eerie. In the dim dusk light, he spotted a woman talking to the two Amish men across the road. A low grunt escaped from his throat when he instantly recognized her and he hastily crossed the road, not hesitating to interrupt them as soon as he was within earshot.

"Excuse me for interrupting gentlemen. Hannah, a word please?" Angus closed his hand over her elbow and ushered her to one side, inviting more than one eyebrow from the two curious-looking men in black.

But Hannah was as resilient and persistent as any newspaper reporter could be and ignored the harsh exit.

"Just the man I was hoping to see," Hannah Jackson started.

"Not gonna happen, Hannah. You know better than to interview my witnesses in an on-going investigation."

"Witnesses? So, they saw the murderer? Have you arrested anyone, Sheriff Reid?" she asked, her tone more official.

Angus merely replied with a squinty grin as he shook his head.

"Come on, Sheriff. Give me something. It's in the interest of the people to know what's happening in their backyard. Can you tell me how Dr. Fisher was murdered?"

"There's nothing to report, Hannah, and we've not ruled it a homicide so don't go writing up false stories in the *Herald* tomorrow. The last thing I need is a town thinking there's a murderer on the loose."

"So, are you saying Dr. Fisher wasn't murdered, Sheriff? Then how did he die? Is Dr. Delaney still with him?" She craned her neck, looking past his tall frame in search of Murphy.

"I know you're just doing your job, Hannah, but please, you know the drill. Until we have facts to substantiate anything, I cannot give you any information about the case. You have my word that you'll get the full story as soon as I know what we're dealing with, okay?"

Hannah rolled her eyes and clipped her pen onto her notebook.

"Not even off the record, Sheriff?"

"Like I said, until the facts say otherwise, I have nothing conclusive to give you at this moment."

"Fine, but I will be printing an initial report in tomorrow's paper, Sheriff. I stand by my viewpoint. The people in Weyport deserve to know that something criminal went down so close to their town."

"This isn't exactly in Weyport's backyard, you know, Hannah. And like I said, I have not concluded it a crime as yet. I prefer you rather don't print anything until we have—"

"I know...the facts. Don't worry, Sheriff, I'll be careful with my words. For now, I'll put out a cultural post on this little town we didn't even know existed. And perhaps something about the Amish community that seems to drive the commerce of this place."

"Fine," Angus agreed. "As long as you stick to the facts in your article. You have my word that you'll get an exclusive if the case suggests otherwise."

"I guess I'll have to take that for now even though my nose tells me something weird is going on in this place. Do we even have a name for this little village, Sheriff?"

"I am very certain I'll know what it is when the morning paper hits my doorstep."

She smiled and started to leave before she looked back and said, "You're sure you don't want to throw me a bone, Sheriff? Even a tiny one? Who knows? I might actually help you catch the killer."

"Nice try, Hannah. I told you, I'm not ruling it a homicide yet so don't go chasing fear into my county okay?"

"If you say so, Sheriff," she said as she walked off.

When she was a safe distance away, Angus turned his attention to the two Amish men who seemed entirely undeterred by his interaction with the pushy reporter.

"My apologies, gentlemen. Sheriff Reid," he introduced himself. "If you don't mind, I'd love to ask you a few questions."

The men nodded in unison, their faces remaining stark and lacking expression. Angus couldn't help but feel uncomfortable by their aloof demeanor.

"Thank you, I won't take up much of your time. Did you know Dr. Fisher?"

"He was our neighbor, and we took care of each other as our Father instructs us," one of them answered.

"Of course. How about today? Did you speak to him at all?"

Both men shook their heads and Angus knew he had to change his questioning if he were to get anything out of them.

"Is this your store?" he asked, looking friendly.

Once more, they shook their heads and a deep frown settled between Angus' eyes.

"It's not your shop?" Angus repeated the question and again it resulted in them shaking their heads.

"Forgive me for asking then, but why have you been

standing here for the past three hours if this isn't your store?"

"We are merely observing, Sheriff Reid. Like I said earlier, Dr. Fisher was our neighbor, and it is God's will that we take care of our neighbors."

Patience was Angus' middle name, but these men were pushing his limits and he had a hard time holding back his frustration. He took a brief pause, then delivered his next question.

"Did either of you notice anything suspicious today?"

The men slowly shook their heads in unison.

"How about any of his patients? Did you happen to see anyone running away from his practice?"

Again, they shook their heads.

"Fine, so nothing or no one suspicious."

Once more, they gestured that they hadn't seen or heard anything.

Angus puffed his cheeks in frustration.

"Would you have told me if you did?"

The men remained silent.

"Didn't think so. So, let me kindly remind you that you could be charged with obstructing an investigation if you intentionally withhold any information. And I'd hate to do that."

The men neatly folded their hands in front of them and for the first time the second one spoke, authority dripping from his voice.

"We are not governed by worldly laws, Sheriff, only

God's law," he said before both tilted their heads in farewell and walked towards the road where their horse-drawn buggy was tied to one of the trees.

When Angus turned around and headed inside the general store, he found a young man behind the single checkout counter in the front of the shop.

"You won't get them to talk, Sheriff. They will never turn on each other," he announced as he came out from behind the counter to restock one of the nearby shelves.

"I thought as much. I take it you're not Amish." Angus asked the man who appeared to be in his early twenties dressed in a pair of dark denim jeans and a t-shirt.

"No way! They have way too many rules. I'm just helping out my grandfather before I head back to New York. I'm Ben, by the way."

"Pleased to meet you, Ben. I'm Sheriff Reid. So, your grandfather owns the store."

"Yup, for as long as I can remember. But he's not doing too well at the moment. Pneumonia or something so I'm just helping out until he's back on his feet."

"I see. I don't suppose you heard or saw anything across the road, did you?"

"Not really, I mean, it's pretty quiet around here most days. They mostly keep to themselves, mind their own business, you know?"

"So, nothing that struck you as odd then."

Jack shrugged his shoulders as he stacked the last batch of black sewing yarn on the shelf.

"Except maybe that girl who came running in here all hot and flustered looking for her mother," he said. "The Amish women are normally quiet and well behaved but this one nearly rang the bell of the door. She's one of the prettier ones." He gave a mischievous smile. "Rachel, I think her name is."

CHAPTER SEVEN

Weyport's salty breeze swept over Caleb Townsend as he strolled along the quaint coastal town's weathered boardwalk. The early morning sun glimmered on the ocean, its golden light lighting up the lookout point as if to lure him in. And he let it, every morning. It was where he went to meet with God. A God he had come to know existed even in solitude, a practice his upbringing strongly opposed. He was taught that faith was found in community, never in isolation. As if access to God was only possible one way. Spending time at the lookout was where his soul was one with creation. He closed his eyes briefly and enjoyed the quiet whispers that wafted off the ocean waves toward him. He loved his solitude and how close it made him feel to God.

Staring out at the ocean, his mind was caught between the teachings of a faith he only ever saw from one point of view, and the haunting questions that had been clouding his mind ever since he first discovered the true passage to heaven didn't come through works or ritualistic traditions. For as long as he could remember, God had taken center stage in his life, ingrained in him since birth. But the God everyone spoke of back then wasn't the God he needed him to be, an English God, not an Amish one.

He couldn't stay. Didn't want to stay. *Rumspringa* had shown him too much. Had opened his eyes to the possibility of a different God. And even if it took him a lifetime to find the intimate faith so many people in Weyport spoke of, he owed it to himself to follow where his heart was leading him.

He recalled the first time he came to Weyport, how daunting it was to go into a world undiscovered. It was the farthest he'd ever been from his family. Ever since he had heard that the town was by the ocean, it was as if something had called out to him, beckoned him to go there. He had never seen an ocean, not even a picture of it, only what his mind conceived from scripture. It was the very ocean God had created, like the one He parted when Moses called out to him. Weyport was everything he yearned for and more, and as far as he was concerned, he never wanted to leave.

But the journey there hadn't been an easy one. He had been forced to choose between the aching in his heart that longed for a life beyond the boundaries of his once Amish life and the future his family expected of him. A future he never wanted. He needed more and yearned to break out from under the rigid religious practices that seemed to do nothing but shackle his soul. And he was prepared to forsake everything for it. His family, his ways, even his last name.

At first, he believed the intimidation that came with years of deep-seated strict guidelines: that he could only earn his place in heaven if he joined the church, that he was sinning against God and his family if he didn't. But the more he pondered about it, the harder his heart fought for freedom until he finally succumbed. As far as he believed, Weyport was where God had destined him to be, where he belonged. He needed to remind himself of that to keep his mind off of what—and who—he had left behind, all in the name of freedom. But there wasn't a day that went by that his conscience wasn't in turmoil over his choice. He often went back and forth with his decision in his head. Weighty matters like those were usually made by the elders, those supposedly closer to God, and according to them, he wasn't equipped to decide for himself. Even today, he questioned if it truly was what God wanted for him. All he knew was what he felt at that moment and that he needed to leave.

The weight of his heritage clung to him, a silent reminder of the stark departure he had made from the Amish life, a departure that now left him at odds with the faith that once defined his every existence.

Weyport was the one place he could explore his faith

freely, where no one knew of his upbringing. Where no one knew he had chosen his last name based on his house being at the edge of town. He hadn't been a Beiler for a while now, didn't feel it belonged anymore, didn't want it to. Nothing about him felt Amish and it needed to stay that way. They didn't want him and he didn't want them. Except for Rachel.

In the beginning he used to meet his only sibling on the bridge that crossed over the river dividing the Amish land from the English land. Until she was caught and shunned. Once again the elders forced him into a decision that made him keep his distance, for Rachel's sake.

He thought about her a lot. They had always gotten on well and sometimes he missed her company, even the company of family. One day, once he found himself, truly found himself in Christ, he would go back to make amends. But not yet.

Pushing the ache in his heart to one side, he let his mind wander to his sister instead. She was so much like him, a free spirited soul whom he was certain would soon want to follow her own destiny. For a while she had tried to persuade him to return, to plead with the elders to take him back. Until the tone of her letters suddenly changed, and they became harder to read. As if she could no longer find reasons for him to go back.

He knew her well enough to know she was holding out on him, but he made a silent vow to never push her into saying more than she was willing to. She was after all breaking the *Ordnung* just by communicating with him, much less engaging in gossip. He could get her shunned for either, or both, again.

Guilt pushed up in the back of his throat like bitter bile and he forced it down as he turned his attention toward the wild ocean instead, its waves crashing onto the rocks below. With the back of his hand, he swept away the lonely tear that had nestled in the corner of his eye before he pulled the collar of his camel-colored winter coat tighter under his chin. His eyes fixed on the waves that mirrored the conflict in his soul. He had thought turning his back on the community would give him the freedom he so desperately needed but all it did was amplify the torture in his soul.

Because crossing the bridge into the world of the English meant he betrayed those he was supposed to protect.

His trembling hands pulled out the last letter he got from Rachel. He had kept it in the inside pocket of his coat, a deliberate decision to keep her close to his heart when he most felt he was all alone in this world.

The corners rustled in the breeze where he was pinching it between his cold fingers. With a gentle touch, he allowed himself to enjoy the purple petals of the single flower that was pressed into the handmade paper before his thumb traced the delicate handwriting, stopping over the last name he only ever saw written on her letters.

Try as he might, he could never ignore opening his

sister's letters. Especially since he knew what it took for Rachel to sneak them to him without being caught. It was another one of the ridiculous rules they had been taught was sinful. As if contact between siblings on opposite sides of the order warranted eternal damnation.

He scoffed then turning the envelope over, parting the paper with two fingers.

The faint scent of lavender escaped from the envelope as he pulled the single sheet of hand pressed paper out. He had read it a million times already, a note he sensed was stained with desperation and despair. His sister's letters had become harder to read. She had stopped writing about the new calves or who had entered into a courtship a few letters ago. Her words were sharper, laced with anger and pain. Once she had even blatantly accused him of betraying her, of not being there for her when she most needed him. Only to ask for forgiveness in the next one. But her words left behind a bitter trail of guilt that he carried with him every day.

As he glimpsed the familiar writing, his eyes picking out scattered words and sentences, his gut twisted in a thousand knots. For in the pit of his stomach dread was settling, as if his sister's cryptic words were ominous harbingers of calamity.

CHAPTER EIGHT

For once, Caleb wished his instincts were wrong, but his suspicions were confirmed the moment he picked up the *Weyport Herald* that lay waiting for him on the curb outside his townhouse.

A single word caught his attention right away and he snatched up the paper. At first, he thought his eyes were deceiving him, that it was a strange trick of his mind. But by the time he reached his kitchen and spread the newspaper open across the white quartz counter, there was no delusion. He scanned the article that took up the entire front page of the *Herald*, his stomach suddenly in knots as he studied the black and white portrait of a man. In fat black letters the heading next to it simply read: Doctor found dead in Amish town.

Surely not. The thought raced across his mind before he focused his attention on the man's photo. His eyes were deep set, a dark almost black color under white bushy brows that matched his long white beard. Something familiar tugged at his memory and he read the caption: Dr. Fisher, chiropractor.

A frown settled on his brow as his eyes went back to the picture, studying the man's face in a desperate attempt to place him. Then, like a lightning bolt it struck him. He knew exactly who this man was. It was the same doctor he had once taken one of his cousins to see, before she and Benjamin were to be married. He remembered it clearly. It was one of the hottest days that summer. His uncle's truck needed a particular engine part and he was sent to collect it at the store. His uncle had asked him to take a few of the women to buy quilting supplies, and his cousin, Rebecca, to an appointment with the chiropractor. He recalled how tense she was on the way there, worse after her appointment when the doctor walked her out.

Caleb's insides trembled as he read the column, pausing on the paragraph emphasizing the mysterious circumstances under which the doctor died.

He pushed the paper to one side, desperate to make sense of the sudden angst that rippled through his body. There was more to the story that nagged at his memory. Fisher... Fisher...the doctor's name echoed in his mind. Until everything inside him froze and sank to the pit of his stomach.

As if a bolt of electricity shot into his legs, Caleb ran up the stairs, his feet navigating the modern polished concrete steps two at a time. From the top of his bedroom closet, he pulled out the shoebox where he kept all his sister's letters. Tossing the contents atop his bed, his shaky fingers sifted through them until he found one of the letters she sent him about three months ago.

Caleb's hands trembled as he slid his finger beneath the loosened wax seal of the letter, the parchment crinkling under his touch. The familiar pretty script of Rachel's handwriting greeted him with an intensity that sent shivers down his spine. He held his breath and began to read, each word piercing his heart like a cold dagger.

"Dearest Caleb," the letter began, "I am writing to you in great fear and desperation. My time here in the Amish community has become unbearable, and for the first time I now know why you had to leave. I wish I had the courage to leave too, before it consumes me. There is darkness all around me, a sinister weight that presses down upon my soul, threatening to suffocate the very life out of me. A life I no longer want."

As Caleb's eyes scanned the words, he could almost hear Rachel's voice, soft and pleading, trembling as if on the verge of tears. The letter detailed how her days had become filled with dread and anxiety, how she found herself constantly feeling unworthy of God's love, fearing who she might become or what she'd need to do to finally be rid of the darkness that imprisoned her soul. It was as if his once warm and happy sister's soul was suddenly covered in a shadowy landscape of secrets and gloom.

His eyes scanned farther down the page.

"The doctor is creepy, and I don't want to see him anymore," she wrote. "His eyes speak of pure evil that I can no longer fight. You have always been my protector, even when we were children, which is why I am writing this letter. Not to burden you, but to ask for your wisdom and prayers. I need to leave this place, to escape the darkness that has taken hold of me every time I see Dr. Fisher. I know it will not be easy, but my faith tells me that there is still hope, and that hope lies with you. Your loving sister in faith and hope." The letter concluded, "Rachel."

Caleb's grip on the letter tightened, his knuckles turning white as he absorbed the desperation in his sister's words. He could feel her fear, her longing for a way out, and it tore at him. The wound threatened to rip him apart. The once peaceful world of their childhood was gone, replaced by an ominous fear she could no longer bear. How did he not see it before? How could he be so self-absorbed and blinded by his stubborn will to shut out his previous life that he abandoned the only person who meant anything to him?

Caleb's heart pounded like a blacksmith's hammer, each beat ringing in his ears as he stared at the words before him. His sister, Rachel—his sweet, innocent sister—was trapped in a web of fear and desperation. She had reached out to him through the letter, hoping that he would catch her cry for help, knowing she was risking everything by asking him for help. His breaths came in short, shallow gasps, as if the weight of her plea was crushing his lungs. Once again, he had let her down, had betrayed their bond, had neglected his duty.

Her desperate words echoed in his mind, playing on an endless loop. He could feel the icy tendrils of dread seeping into his very soul, threatening to swallow him whole.

But beneath it all burned a fierce, unwavering loyalty —a bond forged in the fires of childhood memories, stronger than any force on earth. And it was this loyalty that would be his guiding light, no matter what darkness lay ahead.

"Rachel," he whispered, his voice trembling with emotion, "I swear to you, I will find a way to help you."

With every ounce of strength he could muster, Caleb fought to steady his shaking hands, straightening the letter that had crumpled between his fingers. The realization settled upon him like a shroud. In order to save his sister, he would have to confront his family and everything he had fought so desperately to leave behind.

"God help me," he murmured, the prayer escaping his lips. "Give me the courage to face what I must, and the strength to protect Rachel from whatever evil threatens her." He drew in a deep breath, "And help me not to lose you in the process."

His determination burned with an intensity that eclipsed even the darkest corners of his fears. For Rachel, he would walk through the fire once more, cross back into the life he had so desperately broken free from, and face the people who turned their back on him. He had abandoned Rachel once before, and that was once too many.

As Caleb's resolve solidified, the air around him seemed to hum with an electrifying energy, as if God Himself had heard his plea and granted him the strength he sought.

He folded the letter carefully and tucked it into his pocket, the words within etched into his very being. For his sister, he would sacrifice everything—even if it meant returning to the very place that had nearly destroyed his soul.

CHAPTER NINE

Angus parked his cruiser at the edge of the narrow country road that led into the Amish community and took in the quiet surroundings. He glanced at the clock on the dashboard. It was early, perhaps too early, he thought as sudden concern over his early timing struck. For a brief moment he thought of waiting until the sun fully rose. On the other hand, he had wrestled all night with the perplexity of the case and that Rachel, the Amish girl, was his only lead at this point. Not to mention that Hannah was one of the most persistent reporters he knew. The story would be splashed all over the *Weyport Herald's* front page and from experience he knew that the townsfolk's tongues would start wagging before lunch rolled around. Time wasn't on his side. The sooner he was able to rule the doctor's death an accident, or better yet, natural, the easier it will be for all.

But deep in the pit of his stomach, an uneasy feeling had already taken root.

He turned his attention back to the humble settlement. In the early morning sunrise, a warm golden glow lit up the landscape with hues of bright yellow, casting long shadows on the idyllic scenery. Modest yet meticulously maintained houses stood in stark contrast to the earthy tones of the last autumn leaves that lay thick beneath the scattered trees. Small wisps of smoke rose from a few chimneys, signaling the start of day and a community already hard at work behind the scenes.

Deciding to leave his vehicle behind, knowing that outside automobiles weren't generally welcome inside the commune, he got out of his vehicle and started walking the short distance to the entrance along the road. The air was crisp, and a thin layer of frost covered the elevated patches in the adjacent fields and pastures as the thick scent of fresh manure drifted toward him. From somewhere afar a rooster was late to the party, his crowing reminding Angus just how simple life on the farm was. For the briefest of moments, it distracted him, memories of his childhood days in Scotland dancing at the back of his mind. Life was simpler then too.

As he approached the entrance marked by the large timber sign that had a single Dutch-like word carved into it, he nervously adjusted his belt before straightening his jacket. Feeling more out of place than he had anticipated, he started towards the heart of the Amish enclave.

This was his first encounter with the Amish outside of the two tightlipped men from the previous night, and from what he learned on the Internet the night before they were a tight-knit community, suspicious of outsiders and protective of their way of life. But Rachel was his only lead so far, and he needed answers.

As he approached, he noticed the curious glances from two young men who were pulling a large wooden cart of hay toward a hungry herd of livestock that was pushing their heads through the wooden fence. He nodded politely, acknowledging the residents as he walked past them. By the time he got to the end of the road, as if the rooster was all that was needed to bring the community to life, about half a dozen young children came storming toward him. An older woman chased after them, directing the kids to a nearby building Angus assumed was their schoolhouse. She stopped to greet him, her eyes curious but guarded.

"Good morning," Angus greeted her then introduced himself before adding, "I'm hoping to speak to a young woman named Rachel, if that's possible, please?"

The woman stared back at him, her eyes narrow with suspicion.

"We have many Rachels here, Sheriff," she replied.

"Right, of course," he fumbled feeling nervous. "It's just, I don't have a last name. All I know is that she was seen in the nearby town yesterday. She had gone with her mother and aunt, I believe."

The woman straightened her apron before one hand went to her hip.

"I don't know anything about that, Sheriff, but I'll take you to see the bishop. You will need to ask him. This way," she said, already hastily leading the way.

When she stopped outside one of the houses, she nodded toward the door.

"Bishop Jedediah is in there with the others. They're having their morning meeting. Please wait here while I call him."

Angus nodded, nerves tightening in his stomach. The same nerves he felt the day before when he met with the two Amish men who stood watch outside the store. The same nerves that whispered in his ears, telling him something was amiss.

As he watched a group of teens quietly walk into the nearby barn, he asked God to calm his spirit, to help him ask the right questions, to give him insight that would help solve the case.

Less than a minute later, the woman was back, followed by a man who looked much like the two men from outside the general store the day before.

The man looked to be in his late sixties, his impenetrable eyes and inscrutable countenance giving little away as he stood before Angus. Moments later, three more similar looking men flanked his sides, and it was obvious to Angus that they were the leaders of the community.

"Sheriff Reid," the bishop eventually acknowledged,

his voice deep and measured. "To what do we owe the pleasure of your visit on such a bright early morning?"

Angus didn't miss the cleverly disguised hint at the bad timing of his visit that was masked by the bishop's friendly words.

"I apologize, Bishop, but it couldn't wait. I'm afraid I'm here on official business."

The men's faces were stern as they waited in silence. Angus shuffled nervously before he continued.

"I'm here about Dr. Fisher's passing. I understand he was quite well known by your community, and I need to ask some questions, particularly about a young girl named Rachel. It is believed that she might have been the last person to see the doctor alive."

The men exchanged glances. The bishop folded his hands in front of him, his expression unreadable.

"Rachel Beiler?" he finally asked, his tone deliberate.

"I'm not sure, Bishop. I understand there are a few women here with the same first name. However, if this Rachel Beiler was indeed the young woman who had an appointment with Dr. Fisher yesterday, then she would be whom I need to speak to yes. Do you know where I might find her, please?"

The bishop glanced at the men beside him, turning his attention back to Angus.

"Sheriff, Rachel Beiler has been missing since yesterday evening. We've searched the community, but there's no sign of her."

Angus' eyebrows furrowed in surprise.

"Missing? Did she leave a note or give any indication of where she might have gone?"

"No. She was helping her mother with evening chores and when they went to check on her later, she was gone," the bishop explained. "We've been praying for her safe return, but as of now, we're in the dark."

The unease was back, this time hitting the core of Angus' chest.

"This complicates things, Bishop. If Rachel Beiler was the last person to have seen Dr. Fisher alive, I definitely need to find her. It's really important. In fact, if I were to assume that she had nothing to do with the doctor's death, she could very well be in grave danger."

CHAPTER TEN

The bishop's eyes narrowed slightly.

"Our community values its privacy. We are cooperative, but we cannot allow an outsider to disrupt our way of life. Sometimes the young ones rebel against the *Ordnung*, but more often than not they return on their own."

Angus sighed, his hands on his hips as he watched the farm come alive around them. Understanding the delicate balance he needed to maintain, his voice was gentle but firm when he spoke.

"I appreciate the concern you have for your community, it's certainly warranted, and I assure you of my utmost respect toward you and your people, but a man was found dead on his floor yesterday. A man who we believe had close ties to this community. Now, while at the present moment we don't have evidence to support that his death was with malicious intentions, we also cannot assume that it wasn't. Until proven otherwise, I have a duty to assume the worst-case scenario, and Rachel might be the only one who can clear it all up. If she has any information about her visit with Dr. Fisher yesterday, it could make all the difference. We already know she had an appointment to see him, and we have a witness who can confirm that she arrived for her appointment. Another witness also told us that she was acting quite out of character afterwards. It is vital that I find her, especially if there's even the slightest chance that foul play was involved. Not to mention the fact that if Rachel Beiler was there, or even saw what happened, she could be at risk of falling victim to the same fate as Dr. Fisher. I can put out the word and have a search party here within the hour, and I'll do my best to minimize any disruption, but I have to speak to Rachel."

Desperation and fear flooded Angus' insides, his suspicions over the doctor's mysterious death growing with each passing second.

The bishop studied Angus' face, his eyes piercing deep into his soul as if to search for answers Angus didn't have. After several moments the bishop finally spoke, reluctance evident in his voice.

"You can speak with Rachel's parents. They might have more insight into her whereabouts."

Angus nodded, grateful that at least his request wasn't refused.

The bishop nodded to a woman who had been waiting in the doorway of the house before he turned and left, his posse of elders in his wake.

The plump woman's face revealed an emotion Angus couldn't quite lay his finger on. Nerves perhaps? Or was it fear? But she wasted no time and set off down the path. Angus rushed after her, jumping to match her energetic pace as they wove between the houses.

Slightly out of breath, Angus needed to seize whatever opportunity he had at his disposal.

"I appreciate you helping me. Do you know the girl?"

The woman shot a fearful glance over her shoulder then dropped her brisk walk to a steadier pace.

"My husband won't appreciate me speaking to you, Sheriff."

"The bishop is your husband?"

She nodded then offered a brief introduction. "Yes, I'm Esther Yoder. My husband, Jedediah has been the bishop for many years now."

"I don't mean to put you in an uncomfortable position Mrs. Yoder, but anything you can tell me about Rachel or the doctor would be very helpful."

She glanced at him sideways, squinting at the sun that hit her face.

"Everyone knows Rachel. She's a lovely girl, young and foolish as they all are at her age, but lovely nonetheless."

"How old is she?"

"She's just turned sixteen, the time when all the girls start their adjustments."

Angus frowned.

"Adjustments? Forgive me, I'm not that familiar with your customs."

The woman stopped abruptly, her eyes darting in all directions before she spoke again. This time with hushed tones.

"Dr. Fisher has been our community's chiropractor for decades, since long before my husband became the bishop. His father started the practice when my mother came of age. His treatments are something the women here have all grown to accept as being part of their marital preparation, and it starts when we turn sixteen. We practice natural home birthing, without any interference from modern medicine; we do whatever we can to ensure everything goes smoothly when the time comes. It has long been advised by the council that Dr. Fisher's treatments minimize birthing complications and in turn, eliminate the need for modern medical intervention. It's just the way it's done around here."

Something in her voice told Angus she didn't agree with it, and he decided to push the topic.

"But you don't agree."

She shot him a stern look before she looked away and started walking again, increasing her pace with even more vigor.

"It doesn't matter what I or any of the other women believe. It's what the *Ordnung* says we should do."

"What about you? Have you ever been to see Dr. Fisher?"

Angus knew he was risking all by asking her, but his instincts were telling him to persist.

Mrs. Yoder stopped, her shoulders bending forward before she took a deep breath and turned to face him.

"Sheriff Reid, around here you don't question the elders and you certainly don't question the *Ordnung*, especially if you are a woman. The men decide and we do as we are told."

Angus nodded, his eyes locked with hers.

"I understand." He paused then asked, "And Rachel was seeing the doctor, correct?"

Her eyes confirmed what Angus already knew when Esther briefly glanced at him then looked away.

Noticing her discomfort, Angus decided to switch gears.

"How long do the women see the doctor for these adjustments?"

"They go as long as it takes, until Dr. Fisher decides to stop their treatment."

Angus detected a sad tone to her voice and was about to dig deeper when they stopped in front of one of the houses. The simple wooden plaque announced that they had arrived at the Beilers' house.

Mrs. Yoder knocked twice, then entered.

Angus followed her inside, the wooden floorboards creaking beneath their weight as they entered a warm and inviting kitchen where the aroma of freshly baked bread lingered in the air. At the small wooden table sat a man who appeared younger than the men Angus just met. Behind him, a slender woman stood quietly to one side, her face showing signs of fatigue, her eyes filled with angst.

Mr. Beiler jumped up from behind the table the moment he saw them; an anguished squeal escaped from Mrs. Beiler's lips.

"No-no, Lydia, there's no need for concern. The sheriff is here to help us find Rachel. Jedediah sent him," Mrs. Yoder said as she rushed to Lydia's side.

"Bishop Jed approved this?" Samuel Beiler said, his thumbs tucked behind his suspenders as if he needed them to hold his arms up.

When Mrs. Yoder nodded, Samuel Beiler quickly reacted by reaching out his hand to greet Angus.

"Lydia, please get the sheriff a cup of coffee." He pulled out one of the chairs and invited Angus to take a seat at the table as he sat down at the head of the table.

"Thank you, Mr. Beiler, and thank you for agreeing to see me."

"You're here to help us find our Rachel, correct? We appreciate anything you can do to bring her back to us," he said urgently. "This isn't like her to not come home. I don't care what anyone says. Rachel's not like the other young ones who run away." He cast a watchful eye in Mrs.

Yoder's direction, which evoked a strained look on her face after which she hurried toward the door.

"I'll be off then. We'll be praying for Rachel's safe return," she said before she left, flashing a faint smile through pursed lips.

The atmosphere turned awkwardly quiet, and Angus caught the unspoken exchange between Rachel's parents, intrigue tugging at his insides.

"What do you mean she's not like the others?" Angus asked, "Does this type of thing happen regularly? Teenagers running away from home?"

Again, there was a silent exchange between them, and Angus was certain he saw a glimmer of warning in Samuel's eyes in the way he looked at his wife.

Whatever the silent exchange between them meant, Lydia ignored it and hurried into one of the chairs at the table. She leaned in across the table, her eyes locked onto Angus' face as she readied herself to tell him.

"Don't, Lydia!" Samuel said, his voice low and commanding.

CHAPTER ELEVEN

Caleb's hands moved with a frantic purpose. The morning light shone through the large windows of his bedroom, casting shadows on the walls as he packed his worn leather duffel bag. Essentials only, just in case he needed to spend a night or two close by—clothes for the colder weather, toiletries, a brand new Bible that he had recently picked up from the bookshop in town.

With his mind focused on the challenges that lay ahead, the words from Rachel's letters danced around in his memory. In a desperate effort to make sense of it all he searched for answers beneath any hidden clues, she may have unknowingly scattered throughout the written messages. His heart ached with each passing moment, imagining the fear she must have felt while penning those desperate pleas.

He was scared too. Going back after all this time was

something he thought he'd never have to do. The elders, his parents, they had all closed the door on him before, made it crystal clear he wasn't welcome there, that he had made his choice.

As he tossed the last few items into his bag, he wondered what the people of Weyport would think when they found out that he used to be Amish. Will they reject him too? Would they see him as an imposter, or worse, a fraud?

He paused, his hands stilling on the worn leather of his shoes. He took a deep breath, steeling himself for what he was about to do. With one last glance around the room, he opened the door and left the one place he had ever truly felt whole.

As Caleb pointed the nose of his car due north of Weyport, his sister occupied his thoughts, questions flooding his mind. What was she running from, or who? What was she hiding? What if they wouldn't let him in to see her?

Caleb's chest tightened with each new question that crossed his mind. His stomach was tense and the overwhelming feelings captured his senses to the point where he almost pulled his car over and turned back. But he kept going, turning to God instead. Prayers echoed in his heart: "Father, stay with Rachel until I reach her, and guide me on this journey, to face my deepest fears, my family, the bishop. Whatever Rachel is hiding, give me the wisdom to help her, and let my parents put their judgement of me aside, just this once, for Rachel."

For a short while his prayers helped, but soon fear ripped through his mind once more. Of seeing those who judged him, of seeing the look in his father's eyes, of running the risk of losing himself all over again.

With every mile that passed, Caleb felt nothing but trepidation. And a dark sense of foreboding he could not shake.

As the minutes passed, the landscape began to change; familiar rolling hills and frost-glazed fields flanked the road. When he neared the community, Caleb could almost feel the weight of fear and uncertainty pressing down upon him, his heart pounding at the thought of what was waiting for him. He pulled his car over onto the side of the road and rolled down his window, desperate for air to unclench his tight chest. The air was heavy with the scent of fresh earth and livestock, its simplicity both comforting and suffocating. He hesitated, uncertain of how he would be received after all these years. Would they turn their back on him again? Would they even recognize him?

In the distance, he spotted the county sheriff's vehicle, parked just outside the property gate and his heart caught in his throat. Why was Sheriff Reid there? Had he already discovered Dr. Fisher's relationship with the community?

His hands gripped the steering wheel tighter, steadying himself for the task ahead as he drove down the country road toward the entrance. He pulled his car up behind Sheriff Reid's truck. A few deep breaths gave him the courage he needed to get out of his car and walk into the community, his eyes looking straight ahead. Familiar sounds of a lively farm strangely brought him comfort, the smell of manure hitting his nostrils. Out of the corner of his eye he spotted a few men coming out of one of the houses and he ducked behind the trunk of a large tree, his breath hitching in his chest. His English clothes made him stick out like a sore thumb. They'd for sure ask him to leave before he got to his parents' house if someone saw him now. And all this would be for nothing. He had to see Rachel, before she did something foolish.

A quick glance from behind the tree told him it was safe to keep moving and he picked up his pace, using trees, buggies, and anything else to conceal his presence. When he finally got close to his parents' house, he dashed the last few yards to their front door and pushed his body right up to the thick wooden post. With a shaky hand, he knocked on the door, praying that Rachel would be the one to answer the door. If she did, he could entirely avoid having to see his parents and he and Rachel could find a quiet place to talk about her letters.

But his hopes were dashed when his mother opened the door, her face turned as white as a sheet when she saw him. The two of them stood in the doorway, quietly staring at each other.

"Who is it, Lydia?" Caleb heard his father's voice echo toward them.

His mother's hand went to her mouth as if she needed to stop herself from speaking. Caleb heard the legs of a heavy wooden chair drag across the timber floor before the creaking floorboards told him his father was about to make himself known. Caleb's heart did a somersault in his stomach moments before his father's face came into full view.

The look in his father's eyes was enough to have Caleb turn and run for the hills. His eyes had the intensity and power of making him feel ten years old again, like he just got caught skipping Sunday service. But Caleb couldn't run, even if he wanted to, his legs feeling like lead beneath him.

A dry patch took shape in the back of Caleb's throat when he opened his mouth to say something, his father's stern look still pinning his legs to the ground.

"You're not welcome here." Samuel Beiler spoke the single sentence that had consumed Caleb's heart since the day he had left their church.

Next to Samuel, Lydia squealed from behind her hands that were still keeping her mouth in check.

Say something, Caleb told himself. *Be a man, take courage, for Rachel,* the small voice in his head continued.

"I don't want trouble. I'm just here to see Rachel," Caleb spoke, his voice firmer than he had intended.

"You have no business here, Caleb, not with me and certainly not with Rachel."

Samuel tried to close the door when Lydia stopped him.

"No, Samuel! He's our son! Is it not enough that we've lost our daughter too?"

His mother's words sent a chill down Caleb's spine.

"What do you mean 'lost our daughter'?" he heard himself ask.

"Leave, Caleb. This is family business," Samuel said again, moving to close the door.

But courage to stand up to his father smothered his fear and Caleb pushed his way through the door and into the house.

CHAPTER TWELVE

Caleb's father didn't fight back. Partly because he was much shorter than Caleb, but most likely because Caleb had seen that Sheriff Reid was there too. He glanced briefly at Angus who had been quietly watching them from the far side of the room. Angus pushed his chair out from behind the table and stood up, confusion written all over his face when he looked at Caleb.

"Caleb?" Angus queried.

"Morning, Sheriff," Caleb replied, his heart now filled with fear about why his local sheriff would be in his estranged parents' house. "What are you doing here?" Caleb asked.

"I should ask you the same question," Angus replied.

"Ignore him, Sheriff, he won't be staying," Samuel interjected.

Lydia's eyes were pleading when she looked at Samuel, her hands now on her throat.

"He should know, Samuel," Caleb heard his mother say.

"Know what? What should I know, Father?" Caleb pressed, inviting an angered stare from his father in return.

Angus turned his gaze to Samuel.

"Father? Caleb's your son?" he asked trying to make sense of it all.

"No, he's not! I don't have a son anymore. Our son died a long time ago." Samuel's icy words filled the room.

Pain stabbed at Caleb's heart and threatened to smash it into pieces once again, but he held steady, his eyes firmly locked with his father's like two stags fighting for territory.

"Samuel, please, stop this!" Lydia pleaded again, her voice heavy with suffering. "Our little girl is lost out there somewhere. Caleb deserves to know. He can help."

Samuel spun around to face his wife.

"Know your place, Lydia. The son we once had does not exist. He's dead to us!"

Lydia gasped with emotional pain but didn't let it go.

"What if someone took her, Samuel? What if Rachel is..." She stopped herself from saying what she feared most.

"Enough!" Samuel's voice echoed through the room, instantly causing his wife to turn into a sobbing mess, her hands covering her face as she ran out and disappeared into the next room.

A million questions flooded Angus' mind, confusion momentarily blocking the words from coming out. Across from him Samuel Beiler and Caleb Townsend stood silent, their eyes locked in a silent dual.

"Why don't we take a seat, Mr. Beiler?" Angus eventually said and pulled out the chair Samuel sat in earlier.

"He's not welcome here. This is my home, and this man has no business here. I welcomed you into my home, in obedience to our bishop, to help us find our daughter. Don't make me regret it," Samuel said, his voice low and strained as he fought to remain controlled.

Angus nodded, heeding the warning before turning back to Caleb.

"Then since I am here in an official capacity, let me ask you this, Caleb: Why *are* you here and how do you know the Beilers?"

Caleb cleared his throat from the sorrow that lay thick in the back of it.

"I didn't mean to deceive you or the town, Sheriff. I just needed to start over. To find a place where I'm not judged for who I am, or who I am supposed to be." His eyes briefly went to his father's face as he said it.

"So, you are their son?" Angus asked, a deep frown etched into his forehead.

Caleb nodded.

Samuel groaned under his breath.

"At least I was once," Caleb quickly added before he offered a quick explanation. "I left the community and its church a long time ago and made Weyport my home. I adopted a different last name so I could start over."

"Because you are ashamed, of us and our faith," Samuel cut in.

Caleb didn't defend his father's hurtful statement and looked away instead.

"What brings you here today, Caleb?" Angus continued before Samuel could cast another accusation.

"My sister, Rachel."

"She's not your sister anymore, Caleb. You should leave," Samuel persisted.

This time Caleb could not hold back.

"Rachel is my sister, and she always will be, like it or not. She is my blood. You might have turned your back on me, but she never did. She's a young woman who's desperate to leave these ridiculous ritualistic laws you hold her to. It's smothering her just as it did me."

"You know nothing about her or our faith. Have you no respect?"

"I have respect, and I have faith! A different faith with a God who doesn't need me to do anything or act a certain way to love me. He loves me even if I'm not perfect, even if I sin, without punishment and without rejection."

The door to the other room creaked open and Lydia came to stand between them, her tear-stained face begging for peace between her husband and the only son they had.

"Can you not see what's happening here, Samuel?" she whispered. "God has brought our son back to us. He's giving us a second chance. Rachel is out there in the cold somewhere. Our focus should be on finding her and bringing her home. Not continuing this senseless feud between the two of you."

Lydia's hand rested on her husband's arm, her eyes pleading for Samuel to set aside his anger. But Samuel's face was stern, his fists clenched by his sides as he turned and walked away without uttering another word as he disappeared into the back room.

When he had shut the door behind him, Lydia turned to Caleb.

"This doesn't mean I'm siding with you, Caleb. What you did was wrong. But I choose to set our differences aside until Rachel is safely home again. Agreed?"

His mother had always been the one who saw things with clarity and wisdom and Caleb nodded in agreement before he asked the question that had been burning at the back of his mind ever since he stepped back into his childhood home.

"What's happened to Rachel? What do you mean she's out there somewhere?"

Feeling it was safe to speak up, Angus said, "I think I can help with that, Caleb. According to your parents she never came home last night."

Caleb's heart skipped a beat as he looked at his mother and she nodded, fresh tears trickling down her cheeks.

"It's true." She sank down in the nearby chair and buried her face in her white apron.

"I don't understand. Where would she be, and since when do you call in outside help in times of crisis?" He glanced at Angus then back at his mother.

"Actually, they didn't," Angus said. "I came here looking to speak with your sister, regarding the death of Dr. Fisher."

Caleb's insides tied into a tight knot since that was the reason he needed to see Rachel too.

"What does Rachel have to do with Dr. Fisher's death?" he asked nonetheless, eager to hear how much Angus knew.

"We believe she was the last one to have seen him alive yesterday."

The knot in Caleb's stomach moved up to his chest.

"Except now she's gone missing," Lydia sobbed.

Angus' eyes narrowed as he studied Caleb's face. The look in Caleb's eyes indicated that Caleb knew more than he was letting on.

"But I'm guessing you know that already, don't you Caleb? Why else would you have come back here, facing the wrath of your family and the community you were once a part of?"

"Because Caleb thrives off of humiliating us, challenging our faith and our church," Samuel's voice cut through the thick air as he emerged from the back room.

CHAPTER THIRTEEN

Hurt sat shallow in Caleb's eyes, telling Angus just how deeply Samuel's words were affecting him. Neither of them said another word, as their tongues would cause any more pain between them.

"If I could have a word with you in private, please, Mr. Beiler," Angus said, breaking through the tension and gesturing for them to step outside.

Samuel briefly hesitated then moved toward the door without saying anything.

When they were outside and alone, Angus turned to face Samuel and said, "I don't know what happened between you and Caleb. It's none of my business and I certainly don't want to complicate matters even more, but I do know that time is of the essence. If we were to look for your daughter, the time to act is now. I would like to call in a search team, since this is a matter of urgency. Last night was particularly cold and if she got lost in the bordering woods, especially if she is injured, she most likely has hypothermia by now. If we are to find her alive," he paused, letting his words sink in before he continued, "then our window for rescuing her is getting smaller by the minute."

Samuel's eyes lingered on the nearby pasture where thin layers of ice coated the surface before he looked up at the gray skies.

"There's a storm brewing," he said nodding, "no more than a few hours away. I'll gather as many men as I can in the meantime. But do what you need to bring my daughter home."

Angus squeezed Samuel's shoulder. "I will do whatever I can, Mr. Beiler. One more thing though. With your permission, I'd like to include Caleb in the search. My instincts are telling me he might know your daughter's whereabouts. Siblings usually do."

Samuel's top lip pulled up on one side, and even under his thick black beard Angus could see the bitter taste his suggestion had left in his mouth.

"I know, it's a lot to ask," Angus said, "but we need all the help we can get to find and save your daughter."

Once more Samuel hesitated before nodding, then turned and walked away, disappearing between the houses.

Angus sighed with relief, dropping his head on his

chest before taking out his mobile phone and dialing Tammy at the office.

"Oh, hi, Sheriff," Tammy's always chipper voice came over the phone. "I have a string of messages for you, the phone hasn't stopped ringing. The whole town is outraged over the Fisher case. Although I will say, I get the sense it has more to do with the Amish community they never knew was so close to us. Oh, and Dr. Delaney's been looking for you too. She says it's urgent."

"She was going to be my next phone call but first things first. Round up a search and rescue crew ASAP and send them to my location. Dr. Fisher's last known witness went missing last night."

"The girl? Rachel, was it?"

"Correct. I'm rounding up a few men from the community in the meantime. It seems there's a storm coming so we don't have much time."

"Consider it done, Sheriff."

They hung up and Angus wasted no time calling Murphy.

"Please tell me your autopsy revealed Dr. Fisher died of old age or something," Angus said the moment Murphy's voice came over the phone.

"I wish!" she exclaimed, her voice laced with exhaustion. "This case has me at my wits end, Angus. Every single test I ran came up clean."

"That's impossible. You mean to tell me that this guy just dropped dead in his practice for no reason?"

"That's exactly what I'm saying. His heart just stopped. No signs of distress, no blocked arteries, aneurisms, nothing. Even the toxicology report is clean. And get this, the man had nothing in his stomach either."

"So, our dinner bet is out the window now too." Angus tried to make light of the situation as he scratched the back of his head.

"Unfortunately for me, it seems like it's a draw. But I'll get you on the next one."

Angus could hear her smiling before her voice changed back to its professional tone.

"I've never actually had a case like this, you know. In nearly twelve years of examining corpses, I have never had a body on the table I could not find the cause of death of, much less one with no stomach contents at all. Usually there's something left in his small intestines at the bare minimum, but not this guy. Judging from his colon being clear too, my guess is his last meal was the night before."

"So, he couldn't have ingested poison either."

"If he did, it would have been in liquid form but the tox report would have indicated that. In fact, I ran it twice, just to be certain. No narcotics either."

Angus took a moment to make sense of it all.

"I'm sorry, Angus," Murphy said. "I'm not giving up though. I'll keep digging until I get something, okay?" She paused then added, "What about forensics? Anything in the house perhaps?"

"So far, nothing, not even a single fingerprint. It's like

the place was wiped clean of any evidence. You saw it for yourself. And now the girl's gone missing too, the only real lead I had to go on."

"You mean the Amish girl, his last patient?"

"Yes, Rachel. And get this - turns out Caleb Townsend's her brother."

Murphy exclaimed a loud 'no' before she spoke.

"Caleb Townsend, as in the real estate attorney who helped you with the purchase of your house?"

"Yup, one and the same. He's here as we speak, and it isn't pretty. Apparently, he left the community, caused a lot of bad blood between him and his parents."

"Sounds like you have your work cut out for you on this one, Angus. Speaking of siblings," she paused, then continued, "I have the results of your ancestry test on my desk if you want to swing by sometime to go through it."

Angus fell silent.

"Hello? You still there?"

"I'm here, sorry. Just digesting what you said."

"What's to digest, Angus? Isn't this what you wanted?"

"It is and then again, I guess it isn't. I just don't know if I want the results, that's all."

"It's what you've been waiting for, remember? This might be the one thing that finally tells you where your brother is, the breakthrough in your decades long search for your missing brother. Why stop now?"

"You're right. This is the closest I've come to finding out if at least Logan is still alive."

"Well, let's stay positive on that, shall we? The results are here whenever you are ready, and if you need me by your side, I'm here for you. In the meantime, I have a cadaver to dissect, and I don't care if I have to slice open every organ in his body, I'm going to find out what killed Dr. Fisher. You just focus on finding this Rachel girl and leave Fisher to me, okay? I'll call you when I have anything new," Murphy added before they ended the call.

CHAPTER FOURTEEN

Angus took a minute to turn his focus back to the case, his heart and thoughts consumed with Murphy's conversation. He had hoped the autopsy would at the very least point to how Dr. Fisher died but all it did was cause him more confusion.

He turned around and took in the workings of the farms around him. The residents seemed happy and content with their way of life, as if they didn't have a care in the world. Yet, just on the other side of the door behind him, Caleb had said life inside the community was stifling his sister just as it had him. That Rachel may have run away just like he did. What could have been so terrible to cause a teenage girl to run away? There were certainly unresolved problems in Caleb's family, but didn't every family have its crosses to bear?

Questions whirled around in Angus' head at a million miles an hour. What if Rachel didn't run away from her Amish life like Caleb did, or even from her family? Was it possible she had accidentally witnessed the mysterious murder of Dr. Fisher? That she knew how he died? What if her running away had nothing to do with Dr. Fisher's death at all, and it was nothing more than him grasping at straws in his desperation to find out how the man died?

Angus rubbed the tense spot at the back of his head that now ached with frustration. No matter how hard he tried to answer the questions that ran wild in his head, he couldn't. He had no evidence to work with, not one shred of it. And he had no way of knowing if Rachel's disappearance had anything at all to do with the doctor's death.

The door to the Beilers' house opened behind him, and he spun around to find Caleb exiting the house, his face grim and his shoulders forward.

"You okay?" Angus asked.

Caleb's hands were on his hips as he stared across the farm, his eyes declaring just how troubled his soul was.

"I don't think I will ever be okay again, Sheriff," he scoffed. "Not that I can recall a time that I've ever been okay, come to think of it."

Angus lay one hand atop Caleb's shoulder.

"I'm sorry things between you and your father are strained. I'm going to pray that God restores your relationship as it should be between a father and a son. I never had that chance; my father passed before I could try. But you still have time, Caleb. Life's too short to hold grudges. Perhaps all that's needed right now is for the two of you to turn the other cheek while we find your sister."

Caleb gave a gentle nod.

"I suppose you're right. Not that I haven't tried reconciling with him before. My father is a stubborn man and he's not one to forget easily."

Angus paused briefly before he dared to ask.

"Not that it's any of my business, Caleb, but what happened between the two of you? I guess why I'm asking is because of the comment you made earlier. You said Rachel probably left for the same reasons you did. What did you mean by that?"

Caleb kicked at a lonely stone that lay at his feet before he answered.

"I shouldn't have said that. I don't know why she ran away, or even if she did run away. I was just frustrated with the whole situation. Just being here again after all this time...it's not easy. The Amish way of serving God is much different from the way I'd like to serve Him. It's, for want of a better word, restrained, restricted by rules and guidelines, rituals. It's just how things are around here. That's not to say it's wrong but I wanted more. That's why I left. I needed space to breathe, to find faith in my own way and time. That's not something that can be done here. My father also had other plans for me. I'm his only son and he wanted me to get married, give him grandchildren, and take over the farm, live here, tucked away in a safe bubble. I wasn't ready for it. It was as if my soul was crying out for something I didn't even know existed. I challenged him, the *Ordnung*, and the elders. I argued every word the bishop preached because I needed it to make sense. They told me I was a bad influence on the others, a demon causing division, and then they kicked me out. I'm surprised I'm even allowed to be here today, that they haven't chased me away."

The words were hard to hear but Angus remained quiet, hoping Caleb would offer something more, something that might tell him where Rachel might be. Except, Caleb didn't and moments later, his father came storming around the corner, a small group of men directly behind him.

Angus felt Caleb's body tense up next to him as the men's cold stares fell upon him. When Samuel stopped, so did his posse.

"We're ready to start the search for my daughter, Sheriff," Samuel said, the tone of his voice delivering the intentional silent stab at Caleb.

Angus glanced at the text message that just popped up on his phone.

"And not a moment too soon," he said. "It appears the search and rescue team just pulled up outside the entrance."

He gave a sideways glance at Caleb whose eyes were pinned to a spot in the clouds.

"We should get going," Caleb said, gesturing with his eyes for them to take note of the dark clouds that lay on the horizon.

"It looks like that storm is pushing toward us," Angus commented. "How long do we have?"

One of the other men answered.

"Two hours tops."

"Let's pray that's all we need then, gentlemen. Come with me."

"You'll need this." Lydia was standing in the door of her house holding out a blue dress. "For the sniffer dogs; it's Rachel's. I read it in a book once."

Lydia ignored the curious stare she got from her husband as Angus took the dress from her hands.

"That's a great idea, Mrs. Beiler, thank you."

He turned and hastily led the group of men to the center of the enclave where his search team and their dogs were waiting for him. After a cursory greeting, Angus brought them up to speed before the team leader jumped into action with instructions.

"If you and your men could spread out and take the south-side of the property, Sheriff, my unit will search the adjoining land. I noticed there's a river bordering the east, between this land and the forest. I'll have the dogs start there, in the event she might have fallen in," the unit manager said.

"No chance that happened, sir," Samuel was quick to say. "My Rachel is forbidden to go anywhere near the river. She wouldn't have ventured that way. She respects our laws." His words were targeted at Caleb.

"With respect, Mr. Beiler," Angus interrupted, "we have to consider that she might have been taken against her will. We need to cover all possible scenarios, just to be sure."

He nodded at the team manager to go ahead and give the order to his squad officer.

"Pass these around." The squad officer held out a box of two-way radios. "If you spot anything, anything at all, press the button on the side and speak into the device like this." He demonstrated then held out the box of radios.

Less than a minute later, the men broke away into their groups. A small gathering of women huddled together in silent prayer a short distance away.

As Angus moved toward Samuel and the other men, Caleb stopped him.

"If you don't mind, Sheriff, I think I'll join the other party. I don't think my father would be too pleased to welcome me into theirs."

Angus nodded in agreement.

"Makes sense. I'll radio if we find anything."

When they split away going in opposite directions, Caleb smiled to himself. Because behind his seemingly heedful request to switch teams and search along the river instead, he was in truth hiding something. He knew exactly where Rachel might be hiding.

Rachel needed him and this time he would be there for her and do whatever it took to keep his sister safe. Even if it meant lying to protect her.

CHAPTER FIFTEEN

Rachel's letter burned like hot coals against Caleb's chest. Her face etched in his memory as he drew close to the narrow wooden bridge on the far side of the property. It's where they used to meet in secret before Rachel got caught and shunned for having had contact with him. The bridge wasn't used at all. It was originally built with the intention of expanding the community onto the adjacent land. Hardly anyone knew it was there. Except for him and Rachel. They had discovered it purely by accident when a sheep went missing and their uncle sent them out to find it. They had never seen the sun glow more beautifully than when they stood on the bridge as the river rushed underneath it and took in the full view of the horizon. Since that day, the two of them had gone there all the time, to get away from the residents, and to watch the sun come up as it painted the sky with its soft orange hues. The memory made his heart ache, and he quickly forced it to the back of his mind. Looking around to see if anyone was nearby, Caleb held back behind a strip of dense trees. He had stealthily broken away from the search party when no one paid any attention to him. In the distance, he heard the search dogs barking and he stopped to listen. Had they found something? Had they found Rachel?

But shortly after, a voice came over his two-way radio announcing that it was a false alarm and that they were to continue with the search. The tense knot in his stomach released just enough for him to breathe normally again. He had to find Rachel first and find out what she knew about the doctor.

When he saw that there was no one around, he moved to the foot of the bridge, his eyes searching for his sister along the way.

"Rachel," he whisper-called a few times, stopping only briefly between calls to listen for her answer.

But aside from the trees' branches above his head bending in the cold breeze and the water flowing fast underneath the bridge, it was dead quiet.

He turned his gaze first upstream then down, studying every inch of the banks on both sides of the small river, desperately hoping to see her huddled under a tree somewhere. When he saw nothing, he decided to cross the bridge and search along the opposite boundary. As he reached the other side of the bridge, his eye spotted something in the water. It had caught onto a pile of twigs that was wedging up against a large rock. At first, he didn't make anything of it since it simply looked like a paper bag, but as he bent to get a better look, something familiar caught his eye. A single bright purple blotch, illuminated by faint rays of sunshine that shone through the trees. His heart skipped a beat as his mind slowly caught up to what he was looking at. Running towards it, Caleb slid down the small embankment as he inched his way through the snowy patches and dense twigs that prevented him from moving faster. When he reached the spot, it was undeniable and he scooped it up with one hand, lifting several wet, soggy sticks along with it. Even with the paper wet and nearly turned to mush along the corners, he knew instantly that it was one of Rachel's letters.

Squatting next to the water's edge, his cold fingers moved faster to remove the debris that clung to the wet paper and didn't want to let go. Frustration built up in Caleb's chest, his heart pounding harder with every second that passed as he struggled to loosen the wet letter from the debris' clutches without it tearing. He briefly looked up, scouring the area across the river to make sure he wasn't being watched.

"Come on!" he exclaimed in a whisper as one of the corners threatened to tear away from the rest of the letter.

Several attempts later he had managed to clear most of the woody residue and waterlogged moss away. But it was a soggy mess that would easily break apart if he tried to open and read it. He loosened the scarf around his neck and wrapped the drenched letter in it, pressing down gently to soak up most of the water before he tucked the parcel into his coat pocket. When he was done, he scanned up and down the sides of the river once more. The letter proved that Rachel had been there recently.

Once more, he called out her name and listened closely before moving a few more yards upstream searching for her footprints in the muddy banks. From somewhere downstream he heard water splashing, then a dog's bark. Male voices murmured in the crisp air, too muffled for him to make out what they were saying over the noise of the nearby water, but they weren't far away. His instincts told him to go towards them and he scrambled up the small slope before crossing back over the bridge. All he could think about was Rachel and that they had found her frozen body floating in the icy water. She must have gone to the bridge, perhaps sat there to write the letter before she slipped and fell in. Guilt overcame him, nearly drowning the little bit of sanity he had left. The men's voices grew louder and soon, between the trees, Caleb could see where the men stood next to the water, two canines by their heels. It took no time at all for Caleb to reach them and when he came close, he noticed something white dangling from the tip of a stick that one of the men held in his hand.

"What is it? Did you find her?" Caleb's slightly panicked voice drifted toward them.

"We don't know for certain yet," the team leader quickly replied when Caleb came to stand next to them. "One of the dogs picked up a scent and led us straight here."

Caleb's stomach turned as his eyes homed in on the dangling piece of cloth. When he spoke, his voice cracked.

"It's a covering, a bonnet. All the girls wear them."

The man beckoned for one of his team members to hand him a plastic zip bag, and Caleb watched as he lowered the bonnet into the bag before he sealed it.

"Scour the area!" he yelled out. "All along the banks on both sides. She can't be far, but we need to hurry. The storm is rolling in. Let's go!"

The man's words echoed in his ears as Caleb watched the search party deploy, two men at a time while the dogs sniffed their way along the banks in search of Rachel's scent. Realizing the dogs might pick up her smell from the letters in his pocket he made sure to stand against the wind, keeping a fair distance from the dogs as he went after them. Above his head the dark clouds grew thick and heavy, reminding them that the storm was imminent. The wind had turned thin and icy, warning of the snowstorm. He could no longer feel his face or the tingling in his hands from the cold water. It was as if his body had gone entirely numb. Except for the dread that lingered in the pit of his stomach. That he could still feel.

If he still had any doubts, finding the bonnet just confirmed his earlier suspicions that Rachel was in trouble and that something horrible had happened to his sister.

CHAPTER SIXTEEN

By the time the first flakes of snow fell to the ground between the leafless trees, there was still no sign of Rachel. It had been nearly four hours of searching; two since they had found her bonnet. The weather had taken a turn for the worse, the light snow now a fierce blizzard.

The search commander's voice rang over the walkie-talkie that dangled from Caleb's hip. He was rounding up his men and calling off the search. Caleb's heart jumped in his chest. "No!" he yelled out to a dead space in front of him then snatched the radio from where he had clipped it onto his belt.

"You can't stop now," he yelled into the receiver. "My sister is out here somewhere! She won't survive another night in this cold. Please! You have to keep the search going," Caleb pushed, desperate to find Rachel by any means necessary.

"I'm sorry, Caleb, I have no choice. The weather has turned and there's no sign of it letting up. I can't risk my men getting caught in these conditions. It's too dangerous. The dogs also need to rest. As soon as the blizzard dies down, we'll pick up where we've left off. But for now my hands are tied," the search leader's voice came back over the walkie.

The radio clicked off and Caleb found himself unable to move. He had taken shelter from the blustering wind behind a tree where it felt his feet were stuck to the layer of snow beneath them.

"Where are you, Rachel?" His voice drifted off in the howling wind.

A sudden gust slammed into his cheek causing him to shut his eyes and cover his face with his arm. The team commander was right; it was ludicrous trying to find anyone in this weather. Yet, he couldn't get himself to turn back and abandon the search. If Rachel had fallen into the river and managed to get out, she'd be nearly frozen by now. He had to keep looking, at least until the sun went down.

Without his scarf around his neck, his ears took a beating from the icy wind, and he pulled his coat's collar higher and over his chin, sheltering his eyes with his hands.

"Rachel!" He continued to shout out, repeating it several times as he kept walking all along the banks of the river.

There was no sign of her anywhere.

Exhausted and bitterly cold, Caleb dropped to his knees, his bare palms stopping him from falling flat onto his face as they scraped against the frozen soil in front of him. The icy grasses and weeds pushed up between his frozen fingers, nearly swallowing his bare hands whole. He couldn't give up, shouldn't give up, he told himself. Not this time, not ever.

Get up! His mind tried to convince his frozen limbs, fighting to stay awake as exhaustion and hypothermia threatened to overtake him. But his arms and legs refused to obey, and he could do nothing but stay in place on all fours, his head hanging forward between his shoulders.

"Caleb!" A voice came toward him from somewhere behind.

"Caleb!" he heard again, this time right beside him as two sets of strong hands wrapped around his armpits and lifted him to his feet. He looked up to find Angus' face in front of him.

"We got you, Caleb. Lean on us," Angus told him, but Caleb argued back.

"No, Sheriff, I can't leave her. We have to keep looking for Rachel," he said, his speech stuttering from his teeth chattering.

"You'll die out here," Angus said. "We have to get you inside. We'll resume the search as soon as the storm dies down, I give you my word."

Caleb wanted to fight them off and keep looking for

Rachel, but he no longer had control over his frozen limbs. Nor did he have control over the thoughts that now plagued him, that his sister was likely somewhere dead and buried beneath the snow.

All he had left was a flicker of hope nestled in a tiny corner in the back of his mind. That hope helped him cling onto the notion that perhaps she had found somewhere to hide from the storm, a hollowed out tree, or a makeshift shelter she'd craftily thrown together. She was smart, and she was a fighter. If anyone could survive, Rachel could.

Caleb let Angus and one of the members of the search team carry him back to safety. The bishop had offered for the search team to bunk together in the small hall the community used for church gatherings on Sundays. Although they were left to sleep on the floor, it was at least dry. In addition to a fire in the fireplace, several cast iron fire caldrons on tripods were also positioned around the open room, providing warmth that instantly enveloped Caleb's face as they placed him on the floor beside one.

"Let's get him some dry clothes," Angus said.

But when one of the men tried to remove Caleb's wet coat, he wrestled against it.

"No, leave it on," Caleb said, his voice as stern as he could make it amidst the shivers.

"You'll get ill if we leave it on," Angus intervened.

"No! I'll be fine."

"It's just your coat, Caleb. I'll hang it up over there, in front of the fire," Angus tried again.

Caleb turned his shivering body away from the two men and shuffled closer to the fireplace.

"It'll dry off soon enough," he mumbled.

"If you insist, my friend," Angus said. "Can I at least persuade you to have a cup of warm soup. Your mother was kind enough to whip us up a pot." Angus pushed a mug of soup under Caleb's nose.

The once familiar staple in his mother's kitchen teased his senses and he closed his hands around the cup.

"Thanks. Sorry for before," he muttered a swift apology to Angus.

"It's fine, I understand. This is all very upsetting. She's your sister. I would have done the same in your shoes."

As the hearty soup started to thaw his body from the inside, allowing life back into his body, so too did the dreaded feeling in his stomach return. After a second helping of chicken and vegetable soup, Caleb felt like talking again. He turned to Angus who sat nearby.

"Do you think she's dead?"

Angus took a brief pause before he answered.

"I'd like to believe she's still alive. We don't even know for sure if the head covering is Rachel's. For all we know the wind could have blown it off a washing line and dragged it into the river. Until the lab confirms it, we just don't know for sure."

But Caleb did. He knew it was his sister's, knew she

had been at the bridge. The letter proved it. He wanted desperately to read it, to see if she had mentioned anything more about her visits to the doctor, if she knew anything about his death.

His hand went quietly to the bulge on the side of his coat where he'd wrapped the wet letter in his scarf and hidden it in his pocket. If only he could dry it out next to the fire. Perhaps once everyone was asleep, he mused.

"No matter what, Caleb, we need to keep hoping and praying that your sister is still alive. We will find her," Angus said as he got to his feet. "You should get some sleep. I'm told the blizzard will be gone by daybreak."

CHAPTER SEVENTEEN

Angus was awakened by a woman's scream. He'd spent the night sitting up against one of the walls and had hardly slept a wink. At first, he thought he was imagining it but when another wailing scream chilled him to the bone, he knew it was real.

Jumping up, he ran to the door to look outside. It was early and the sun had just poked its first rays through the clouds. Several early risers had heard the screams too and were running down towards one of the barns. Angus trailed behind to where a small group of men, women, and older children stood huddled outside the barn door, guarded by two middle-aged farmers.

"What's going on?" Angus asked when he found his way to the front of the huddle.

The two Amish men exchanged looks before one answered.

"One of our men, well, he's no longer with us," he said struggling to find the words.

"He's dead?" Angus clarified to which they both nodded.

"Do you know what happened?" Angus pressed.

"We don't know, Sheriff, but it's not very pleasing to the eye. Bishop Yoder and a few of the elders are inside. It's better to leave them be."

"Not if the man was murdered," Angus said sternly sending gasps through the small gathering behind him.

The way the two farmers' eyes doubled in size told Angus they were as shocked by his statement as the onlookers behind him.

"Let me through, please, gentlemen," he added.

Without uttering another word, the men parted like the Red Sea and opened the barn door for Angus to enter. The moment he stepped inside and the doors closed again behind him, Bishop Yoder's voice bellowed toward him.

"With respect, Sheriff, this matter doesn't concern you," he said as he hurried toward Angus.

"The respect is mutual, Bishop. However, this community does fall within my jurisdiction. As the county sheriff this is very much my business."

The bishop shook his head, his face stern.

"We deal with these matters privately. This is a working farm and accidents happen."

Angus felt the frustration push harder into his already half-clenched fists.

"If indeed it was an accident, I'd like to make my own assessment, " Angus said then walked toward where the elders were blocking him from seeing the corpse on the floor behind them.

"Kindly ask your men to step away from the body," Angus instructed when he was stopped by men whose eyes looked as stern as the bishop's. When they didn't move, Angus held a firm gaze as he waited for the bishop to comply. The bishop must have gestured for them to step aside because moments later they cleared the way. Angus saw that the dead body on the floor beside them looked strikingly similar to that of Dr. Fisher's.

It was all Angus needed to instantly know that whoever was laying on the floor in front of him had died in the exact way the doctor had and that all evidence was now pointing to the fact that Dr. Fisher had been murdered. But what was even clearer to Angus was that he now had two mysterious murders on his hands with no known cause of death.

"Gentlemen, I am sorry to inform you," Angus started as he turned to face the bishop, "that this was no accident. This man was murdered. I'm going to need you to step outside and prepare yourselves for a little bit of disruption around here as we further investigate the matter."

"How could you know for certain that he was killed? Looks to me like he had a stroke. It happens," the bishop argued.

"Actually, I do know for a fact that this man was

murdered because this is precisely how we found Dr. Fisher two days ago."

The men murmured amongst each other as Angus shared the information. They moved to one side and listened as the bishop spoke to them in hushed tones. When he turned back to face Angus his voice was calm.

"Whatever you need to find out who did this, Sheriff, you have our full support. All I ask is that you keep me informed and allow me to convey the news to his wife and children. And if at all possible, keep the disruption to the minimum, please."

Angus nodded, his mind already on the magnitude of the situation.

"I'll try my utmost, Bishop, but in the meantime, I would appreciate if you could lock down the community as soon as possible. I don't want anyone coming in or leaving. Also, I will need to speak to whoever found him so if you can point that person out to me, please, I would appreciate it."

The bishop nodded in agreement and proceeded toward the exit, his men in step behind him.

"They're outside, two of our younger adults who came in to do their chores this morning."

Angus followed him to where the bishop pointed at two youths no more than twenty years old, sitting to one side on a bale of hay.

"One last thing, Bishop. I'm going to need the victim's name, please." Angus had his black pocketbook in hand.

"Jonathan Lapp. He lived a few houses over from that paddock over there. Now if you'll excuse us, Sheriff, I have to pay his family a visit."

"Thank you. If you can let Mrs. Lapp know, I'll be popping around myself in a little while. We do still have a missing girl to find so as soon as the search party heads off, I'll be stopping by to see her."

The bishop's forehead drew into a deep frown.

"Do you think Rachel had something to do with Brother Lapp's death? Is that why she ran away?"

"I wouldn't be so quick to jump to any conclusions about Rachel. At this point, we don't know for a fact that she did run away. We found what we believe is her head covering in the stream so it's entirely possible that she could have slipped and fallen into the water. We're hopeful that she might have found shelter from the storm last night and that we will locate her today."

Satisfied with that answer, the bishop and his men left and Angus called his office to report the incident.

His thoughts were consumed by the events that had taken place and he quickly sent a text message to the rescue team telling them to start Rachel's search without him. This case now demanded all of his attention.

Angus walked over to the pair of youths who had found Mr. Lapp's body in the barn where they sat waiting for him between stacks of hay bales. The boy, no older than twenty, sat with his head in his hands while the girl, who strangely matched him in both age and appearance, sat fiddling with her fingers in her lap.

"Hi, I'm Sheriff Reid. You can call me Angus if you'd like," Angus said when the young man with the boyish face looked up at him.

"I'm Timmy," he replied. "This is my sister, Justine."

"We're twins," she added when Angus' face revealed his curiosity.

"That explains it," Angus smiled. "Mind if I ask you a few questions?"

The youngsters shook their heads in unison.

"Can you tell me what happened - how it came that you found Mr. Lapp?"

"There's not much to say. We went in at five to fetch fresh fodder and he was just laying there, all curled up with his eyes—" Timmy dropped his head between his shoulders again.

"Did you see or hear anything or anyone else when you went in?"

Timmy's eyes grew big.

"I thought it was a stroke or something. Did someone do this to him?" he asked, looking shocked.

"That's what I'm trying to establish. So, did you hear or see anything strange when you went in this morning?"

Once more, they both shook their heads.

"Only—" Timmy started saying then stopped.

"Only what, Timmy?"

"The footprints in the snow when we first walked up to the barn. I thought it was strange, that's all."

"And why is that?"

"Because they were coming out of the barn, not going in. I just thought it was strange considering we had all this snow last night so someone must have come out of the barn just before we got there."

CHAPTER EIGHTEEN

Timmy's astute observation made Angus promptly look over his shoulder at the barn, his eyes scanning the area in front of the door. The ground had turned to a muddy slush as a result of the foot traffic from the onlookers and others that had already entered the barn. He hurried to the barn's entrance, disappointment surging through him as he took a closer look. He was careless. He should have known to protect the area sooner, he thought, biting down on his bottom lip. When he turned and walked back to the twins, he prayed the oversight wouldn't be one he would come to regret.

"Can I borrow some of these hay bales, please?" he asked the twins, pointing to the stacks next to them.

They nodded without hesitation then watched as Angus used them to cordon off the entire section in front of the barn door.

"Is there any other way in or out of the barn?" he asked when he had finished.

"Not unless you're able to climb up through the vent window," Justine said as she pointed toward the small opening high above the barn doors.

"I guess that means you would need a ladder to get up there, and since it would be nearly impossible for that to go unnoticed, I'll take that as a no," Angus said.

"I don't suppose you might know why Mr. Lapp was in the barn to begin with."

"Well, it is his barn," Timmy said pulling his shoulders to his ears.

"I see. Is he normally in this early, before you?"

Justine shook her head.

"Never. That's our job, to open up and distribute the animal feed. He usually comes after breakfast."

"What about at the end of the day?" Angus continued his questioning.

Once again, the twins responded at the same time by shrugging their shoulders.

"One last question. When was the last time you saw or spoke to Mr. Lapp?"

They looked at each other.

"Sometime yesterday just before lunch, if I had to guess," Timmy answered.

"Thanks, you've been very helpful. I'm sorry you had to see him like this," Angus said. "If you think of anything else, please let me know."

The pair nodded then hurried off to where their friends stood waiting for them to one side. Angus turned his attention back to the barn and the prints in the snow. It would be nearly impossible to retrieve any distinct footprints from the area directly in front of the barn, so he walked along the side of the barn toward the back, surveying the immediate area. Behind the barn, the snow was entirely untouched, likely due to it backing onto a large paddock that stretched all the way down to the river. He lingered there for a while, scanning every inch of the snowy ground. As he turned the corner to head back up along the other side, he spotted the faint set of footprints leading from the paddock's fence along the other side of the barn to where they ran right in front of the doors. Joy flooded his heart and made it jump inside his chest as a wide smile settled onto his face.

"I take it you found something significant for you to be smiling like that," Murphy commented as she approached him.

"It's that obvious, huh?" Angus replied. He ordered two of his deputies to tape off the entire area around the barn, pointing out the footprints he had found running between the barn and the paddock.

"So, care to share why you dragged me all the way out here before I've had my morning coffee?"

Angus leaned in.

"I promise I'll make it up to you when all this is done, okay?"

Murphy's sweet smile sent a bolt of electricity into his stomach. He cleared his throat to adjust his focus back onto the case.

"We've got ourselves another body, Dr. Delaney," he said.

"I assumed that was why I was called here." Her eyes were playful.

"And guess what?" His voice was teasing.

"Okay, I'll play. What?"

"He died in precisely the same manner as our chiropractor did." Angus waited for Murphy to digest the information.

"And you know this how?"

"Well, come see for yourself, but I reckon we have a double murder on our hands, and by the look of it, my guess is it was committed by the same person."

Murphy cocked her head, one brow lifting into a question mark.

"Right. How about I let your expert opinion assess the situation instead?" Angus replied quickly, smiling.

"After you, Dr. Delaney," he added as he gestured Murphy into the barn, instructing the forensics unit to focus on the footprints before he followed her in. When he and Murphy stood over the body, the questions and skepticism in Murphy's face vanished in an instant.

"It pains me to say this, but it looks as if you are right, Angus."

She knelt down next to the corpse, putting on her latex gloves before she pulled away his eyelids.

"No hemorrhaging either," she reported rhetorically before engaging in a series of smaller tests.

"Wait," she said stopping halfway through checking the cadaver's liver's temperature. "Are you saying we're dealing with a serial killer here, Angus?"

"Whoa, I won't go that far, at least not yet. The body count needs to be three at minimum before we label it as such. Although I will say that the similarities are uncanny. And all I have, is one set of footprints leading up to the barn. That's it. No murder weapon or COD."

"And I'm afraid I can't say anything to help in that regard either. Dr. Fisher's autopsy has come up empty so far, and at quick glance, it seems the results will be the same with this guy."

Angus scratched the back of his head.

"This can't be happening, Murphy. I mean, two bodies less than forty-eight hours apart with what seems to be the same modus operandi."

"Not to mention the obvious Amish connection," Murphy added.

"What are we missing here, Murph? Without a COD I have no direction to follow."

"There is a silver lining with us having two victims though."

"Really? I'm all ears."

"Well, my examination will now reveal anomalies, and that's what we want."

"I don't follow," Angus said, frowning.

"It's a simple case of comparison. Two bodies, side by side, with the same test results. Instead of looking for similarities to tie the two cases together, I'll be looking for abnormalities, anything that deviates from the norm and compare those. If I can spot the same inconsistency in both examinations, it might bring us closer to our cause of death."

Angus smiled as he crossed his arms.

"That's really smart, Murphy."

"In the meantime, I can give you a time of death on this guy if you'd like. Although, it was pretty cold last night so we might be off by about an hour or so."

"I'll bear that in mind," Angus said.

Murphy hovered over the corpse, paused, then said, "Two, maybe three hours."

"That's interesting," Angus commented right away.

"Why's that?" Murphy asked as she stood up and pulled off her gloves.

"Because it was barely snowing at around three thirty a.m. I know because I woke up from Caleb bumping up against the furnace in the room. I happened to look out the window and saw that it wasn't snowing as much. In fact, it had pretty nearly stopped altogether."

"Okay, still don't get why you find that intriguing."

"Because the kids who had found the body said they

came in at five a.m. and noticed footprints leading *out* of the barn. I also found fresh footprints next to the barn, running from the barn to the paddock."

"That means that the murder took place between three thirty and five a.m.," Murphy confirmed. "That's a great piece of information so why aren't you smiling?"

Angus rubbed two fingers across his forehead.

"Because the footprints I found indicate a small shoe size, most likely a female's and the direction they went just so happened to also be where they found a bonnet that we believe belongs to Rachel, Caleb's sister."

CHAPTER NINETEEN

Caleb cast a watchful eye across the makeshift bunk room where they had all taken shelter from the storm the night before. He'd spent all night carefully drying out Rachel's letter in front of the fire while everyone was asleep, and very nearly got caught when Angus woke up while he added more wood to the fireplace.

With the sheriff's attention occupied with whatever it was that had him running out in such a hurry a short while ago, he had the perfect opportunity to read the letter he found in the river the day before. He waited for the right moment, keeping his eye on the search party's leader on the other side of the room where he was briefing his crew —they were getting ready to restart the search. If he were to find Rachel first, he had to see what was in her letter, just in case she might have said where she was going. He glanced at the men standing on the other side of the room, their attention on their leader's instructions. Now was his chance, Caleb thought, and carefully took the letter from where his scarf was covering it on the floor next to him. The corners of the single folded page were stuck together, and he gently slid his pocketknife between the parchment to break them apart. He slowly unwrapped the letter, peeling away the bright bluish blotches that glued the letter together in several places where the ink had run into the paper. When the paper came apart and opened up, it revealed several smudged words that were now completely illegible. Hope sank into the pit of his stomach. A quick scan of the words around the ink stains made no sense on their own and he brought the letter closer to his eyes to study more closely. But it was entirely useless; the blotches of ink covered all but a few insignificant sentences.

Behind him, one of the dogs suddenly barked and gave Caleb a fright that made him nearly tear off a chunk of the fragile paper. The dog didn't let up and Caleb turned around to look at it, instantly realizing that the dog's attention was pinned solely on him—and Rachel's letter. How careless, he thought, as he realized the dog must be picking up on his sister's scent. He hurriedly wrapped the letter between the layers of his scarf before he tucked it under his armpit inside his jacket. When the moment presented itself again, he'd have another go at it, he decided. For a moment, he contemplated showing it to the search commander since there was nothing of significance in the letter but mostly because he was desperate to find Rachel alive. But as he stood up to act upon the notion, he overheard the team leader informing his squad that a body had just been discovered in a nearby barn.

Caleb's insides dropped to his feet, his mind working through the news. What if it was Rachel, the thought rushed through his mind.

"What was that about a body?" he anxiously yelled across the room as he hurried over to where the team stood huddled around their leader.

When he got close, the dogs frantically barked at him, bringing him to an abrupt stop. The handler's eyes darted between the dog and Caleb before it settled on his commanding officer's curious stare.

Caleb's body tensed up, his arm pinned to his side and onto the concealed letter inside his jacket. He didn't like dogs even when they were well-behaved and these two search dogs sent his fear into overdrive. His eyes went to their handlers who were trying to calm their dogs, but they kept barking, their bodies straining against their leashes as they tried to go toward Caleb.

Taking several steps back toward the exit, his eyes never left the dogs.

"Call them off!" he eventually yelled at the handlers.

But the commanding officer's suspicious glare stuck to his face like glue when he asked the question Caleb knew would come.

"They're picking up your sister's scent, Caleb. Is there anything you need to tell me?"

Caleb's mind ran wild in a desperate attempt to come up with something to say.

"They're detecting something of Rachel's, Caleb. If I cut them loose, they'll go straight to it. So, I'm going to ask you again, do you have anything of Rachel's? Do you know or have something of hers that will help us find her?"

Caleb's eyes were wide, his heart thumping against his chest. He didn't want to lie. He wanted to protect his sister and make sure she wasn't in any trouble.

"It's nothing," he quickly answered. "Just an old letter of hers I have in my jacket. I carry it with me, to keep her close to me."

His hand moved to retrieve the last letter she sent to him, hoping it would throw the dogs off the one he had found in the river. When he handed it to the commanding officer, the dogs' noses followed it. Moments later the handlers patted the dogs' heads, and when they instantly settled down, Caleb knew his diversion had worked.

"See, it's just an old letter she sent me," Caleb said to make sure they believed him.

Suddenly conscious of someone standing behind him, Caleb turned to look and saw his father's stern face right behind him.

A jolt of nerves rushed through his chest as his father's eyes revealed his thoughts, his glance darting back and forth between Rachel's letter and Caleb's eyes.

The atmosphere between them was thick with tension that rendered Caleb speechless under his father's angry eyes.

"You are an even bigger traitor than I thought," Samuel's voice came at him, calmer than Caleb had expected to hear.

"You left us no alternative, Father," Caleb replied in nearly hushed tones.

"It was never my choice, Caleb. You have yourself to thank for that. You chose to turn your back on us, remember? And still your respect for this community and your family ceases to exist. I want you to leave and never come back. Do you hear me? You are no longer my son, and you don't get to call me your father. Get off our land. Rachel doesn't concern you."

Samuel's words were final as he pushed past Caleb to grab the box of two-way radios from the chair beside the team leader.

His callous words cut deep into the already opened wounds of Caleb's heart.

"I have as much right to be part of this search as any of these men here," Caleb told his father who now stood with his back turned to him.

Samuel spun around, his eyes darker than Caleb had ever seen them.

"Leave, Caleb!"

Something in his father's voice told Caleb that he had pushed him beyond what little self-control he still had in his presence, and he took back the letter from the search party commander before he turned and left.

When the sun's early rays fell upon Caleb's face, sorrow lay shallow in his throat. Somehow, he had thought that his coming could fix what was broken between him and his family. That time would have healed his father's anger towards him. But he was wrong. As far as his father was concerned, he was no longer his son.

And with Rachel now gone, possibly forever, there was nothing else left to fight for.

With his heart numbed by his father's harsh words, Caleb was intent on never returning there again, and set off in the direction of his car. But as he walked past the commotion outside Mr. Lapp's barn and he saw the coroner wheel away a body atop a gurney, he knew he could never give up on his sister. Nor should he.

As if a mighty wind propelled his body, Caleb ran across the snow toward the covered corpse.

CHAPTER TWENTY

From the corner of his eye, Angus spotted Caleb darting toward the coroner's vehicle, his gaze fixed on the gurney. It took no time to realize what he was about to do, and Angus moved to stop him.

"Stop! You can't touch him, Caleb!" Angus yelled just in time.

Caleb stopped and looked back at Angus, his eyes questioning as he spoke.

"Him? It's not Rachel?"

Angus was next to him and shook his head.

"No, it's not. It's not Rachel."

Caleb's gaze went back to the body as they loaded it in the back of the coroner's van.

"Then who is it?" Confusion mixed with relief washed into Caleb's face.

"His name was Jonathan Lapp. Did you know him?"

Caleb nodded.

"He was friends with my father."

Angus paused, his voice low when he asked his next question.

"What about Rachel? Did she know him?"

Caleb's eyes saw the suspicious look in Angus' eyes, and he cocked his head slightly when he replied.

"Why do you ask, Sheriff? What does Rachel knowing Mr. Lapp have anything to do with him being dead? My sister is missing, possibly next in line to end up dead. Why aren't you out there looking for her?"

"That's what I'm trying to do here, Caleb."

"No, you're not. You're interrogating me, asking me all sorts of idiotic questions about Jonathan Lapp when my sixteen year old sister is still out there in the cold." Caleb was near panic as he paced back and forth with frustration. "I have to find her," he said almost to himself.

"I'd like nothing more, Caleb. That's why my men are ready to get out there and look for her again. You need to keep your head straight if we're going to have any chance of finding her. I know it's hard and you feel frustrated that there's not more you can do, but right now the best thing is to keep your wits about you." Angus paused, assessing if his pep talk had any effect on Caleb. When Caleb stopped pacing, Angus placed his hand on top of Caleb's shoulder.

"The more men we have out there looking for her the better, so I suggest you put all this energy into the search and join the team instead."

Caleb looked away.

"I can't. My father chased me away. I'm not welcome here anymore, Sheriff." Caleb's voice cracked as he spoke the words aloud.

"I'm not sure what happened between you and your father, Caleb, but I'm going to pray God works a miracle in your hearts. In the meantime, I have a missing teenage girl and a killer to catch, and I could use all the help I can get right now."

Caleb's eyebrows pulled into a frown.

"A killer? What do you mean you're looking for a killer?" Caleb asked.

Angus didn't answer, his mind searching for what to say next.

"I just assumed that Mr. Lapp had an accident, being a farmer and all, and how is this even related to Rachel being missing?" Caleb asked, then rambled off a string of questions without giving Angus a chance to answer any of them. "Wait! Does Jonathan Lapp's death have anything to do with Dr. Fisher's death? Is Rachel in some kind of trouble? You have to tell me, Sheriff!" Caleb's voice was near frantic, his eyes pleading as his gaze searched Angus' face.

Unable to avoid the barrage of questions Caleb was throwing at him, Angus decided to drop his guard and trust his heart. He knew he was taking a risk, but his options were limited and this particular situation called for him to step outside the lines of the rulebook.

"I want to show you something," Angus said.

Caleb nodded eagerly, his eyebrows raised.

Angus led the way around the barn to where he had found the footprints that headed toward the river.

"I found these earlier. Do you know why someone would be in the barn before 5 a.m. chores only to then leave by crossing through the paddock?"

Angus studied Caleb's face as his eyes traced the set of footprints across the snowy paddock. The look in Caleb's eyes hinted that he knew something.

"Do you know whose footprints these are, Caleb?" Angus pressed for an answer.

But Caleb didn't respond, his eyes remained fixed on the trail that ran through the paddock to where it eventually disappeared between the trees.

"I have to go," Caleb suddenly replied, pushing his hands deeper into the pockets of his jeans.

"If you know anything, now's your chance to tell me," Angus said, his instincts telling him that Caleb was hiding something.

"I don't know anything, and I have no idea where my sister is or why she left. I have to go." Caleb turned to leave when Angus stopped him.

"It looks like a woman's shoe size, Caleb. Do you think these shoe impressions belong to Rachel?"

Caleb's stunned face said it all.

"I don't know how these footprints got here or why they're here. All I know is that my sister is missing and for all we know, she might be the killer's next target. I have to go; I have to find her, before it's too late."

Caleb spun around and hurried to where the search unit had started breaking into small groups to resume the search. Angus let him go, his gaze back on the set of prints in the snow as his mind worked through the details of the homicide cases.

Perhaps Rachel was innocent, even in danger as Caleb suggested. Only he somehow couldn't get past the fact that the killer's modus operandi for the two victims didn't align with a reason as to why anyone would want a young girl dead. His victims were both male and in their sixties. Their only connection was that they had access to Rachel, either in a professional capacity or via her family. But that could just be pure coincidence. Beyond that, there wasn't a single shred of evidence that suggested Rachel might be the killer's next target. All he knew for certain was that both victims seemed to have died in the same manner and that there was no denying that the prints in the snow likely belonged to a woman.

As Angus stared out across the snow-covered paddock, one thing became crystal clear; following the prints was his only recourse. He lifted the crime scene tape over his head and stepped into the paddock, the soft snow sinking beneath his weight.

As he walked alongside the tracks, he studied the impressions, stopping every few yards where the crime lab's markers pointed out each step to take a closer look.

The length between each impression was smaller than his. It had to have been made by a woman and she was definitely walking; running would have made the strides as long as his. The impressions were also not as deep as his, further proof that the person was smaller in frame. With every passing step he became more certain that they belonged to Rachel. Perhaps she had been hiding out in the barn all along or came back and discovered the body before the twins got there. Or worse, was the one who committed both murders.

When he got to the edge of the land, the tracks faded between the trees. He stopped, his heart beating wild in his chest. Desperate to pick up the trail, he scanned the small open spaces between the tall trees but saw no more. He was about to continue down to the river through the trees when his mobile phone vibrated against his hip.

"I'm praying you called to tell me you found something," he said when he saw the incoming call was from Murphy.

"God must be listening because I think I have!" Murphy's voice was buzzing with excitement in his ear. "I think I found our murder weapon, Angus," she added.

CHAPTER TWENTY-ONE

Angus felt his stomach jump with excitement as Murphy's words rang in his ear.

"I think you meant to say that you found our cause of death but still, I'm all ears," he replied.

"No, no, there's no mistake. You heard correctly," Murphy said. "I found our murder weapon." She giggled with glee before she continued. "In actual fact, it's *both* our weapon *and* our cause of death."

Angus rubbed the mounting tension at the back of his neck.

"Murphy, I hardly slept a wink last night and haven't had my coffee either so, if you're trying to confuse me, you're succeeding at it."

Murphy's excitement was palpable even over the telephone.

"Fine, I'll just come out and say it but brace yourself,

Angus. Never in all my years have I had a case that excited me more. I mean, this is unheard of."

She was animated and Angus could almost hear her pacing her office floor.

"You say that with every case, Murph," Angus laughed. "But seriously, just tell me already. I'm dying a slow and painful death over here."

"They were poisoned, Angus, poisoned! And it's not arsenic or even cyanide. I mean, it's what spy novels are made of!"

Angus cradled the back of his neck as he tried to make sense of Murphy's statements.

"Did you hear me, Angus?"

"Oh, I definitely heard you, Murph, I just don't know what to make of it to be honest. You have my head spinning."

"I know, right? It's insane. I've read about arsenic cases in my journals. They're rare in homicides nowadays because our technology has caught up since its prevalence in the Victorian era. But even still, it remains the most obvious of poisons if you're thinking of killing someone. So of course, it was the first poison I tested. But here's where it gets interesting. When I didn't detect any internal bleeding or skin rashes, I ruled it out, naturally."

"Naturally," Angus mocked, thoroughly enjoying the passion she had for her job.

"And needless to say, I immediately went ahead and ran tests for all the other common poisons like cyanide,

Botox, belladonna, you name it. But the tests all came back negative. I'll admit, it had me stumped because having eliminated every other possible cause of death, murder by poison was my only running theory. I was just about to give up when it hit me like a ton of bricks in the middle of the night. Just last month I happened to pick up an old copy of National Geographic and I recalled this article I had read. And wouldn't you guess it, I still had it in my desk drawer. There it was, right in front of me, this two-page spread on the Amazonian Indians." She squealed with excitement.

"I'm guessing all this is going somewhere, but I'm kind of in the middle of something," Angus nudged feeling slightly agitated.

"Yes, sorry, it's just so exciting. I'll explain. The Amazonian Indians extract a neurotoxin from the skin of a frog, aptly named the Golden Dart frog. They then apply the neurotoxin to the tips of the darts they use for hunting. These frogs are no bigger than our thumbs but just the smallest amount of venom from them is enough to kill ten people! Wanna know the best part?" she continued without waiting for Angus to answer. "The venom causes paralysis and cardiac arrest, killing its prey within minutes." She squealed again.

"So, we're looking for an Amazonian frog. That's our murderer," Angus said with less enthusiasm as his eyes scanned the ground around his feet as if to find the frog.

"I know, it's farfetched, and I did say to brace yourself,

but honestly Angus, it makes perfect sense. In fact, it's the only plausible explanation I have at this stage. I really do think it's what killed both our victims."

"I don't know, Murphy, it seems highly unlikely if I'm honest. I mean, a frog, from the Amazon no less. I don't even know how it is possible for Amazonian frogs to live in this climate. Not to mention the fact that we're now saying there's a chance both of these men died from a rare toxic frog." Angus rubbed his tired eyes, frustration coursing through his veins before he spoke again.

"Say we work with this theory of yours. Is there any way to back it up with a blood test or something?"

Murphy sighed, the tone of her voice suddenly less enthusiastic.

"Unfortunately, that's where the problem comes in. I have no way of testing it. Obviously, it's too rare a toxin for its composition to be recorded in our database and without a specimen to compare with, I don't know what to look for in our victims' blood."

Angus groaned throwing his head back, lifting his gaze to the clouds above the trees.

"It's like finding a needle in a haystack, Murphy. I never thought I'd say it, but I've never felt more lost in a case."

"I wish there was something more I could say, but right now, my gut is telling me this is worth looking into. Perhaps one of the kids in the community has seen a frog somewhere, down by the river perhaps. You know, kids explore the strangest places when they grow up in open spaces like they have there. In the meantime, I'm going to see if I can track down a herpetologist through one of my old college professors. If I can get my hands on the chemical structure of batrachotoxin, I'll be able to confirm COD, or not. It just won't be quick so don't stop praying for that miracle, okay."

When she hung up Angus felt the weight of the investigation pushing down on his chest. He had investigated many homicides but this one took the cake. He needed a break in these cases before word got out. And he needed sleep.

He pinched the bridge of his nose before switching his cell phone's screen to the internet search page. He typed 'golden dart frog' in the search bar, snorting at how insane it sounded as he waited for the results.

An image of a bright yellow frog popped up on the screen, its name, Golden Dart frog, in the caption. As he scanned through the article next to the image, it confirmed everything Murphy had told him, right down to where it showed an image of a Columbian hunter shooting a poisoned dart through a blowgun.

Angus scrolled through the information. He desperately wanted to believe Murphy's theory, but if a dart killed either of the victims, surely she would have found the entry point on their bodies. Which meant that the only way these men could have been poisoned was by coming in contact with the venom itself.

Switching the screen off, Angus cast his sights on the stream that ran just beyond the trees. He then glanced back to the shoe prints that led from the barn behind him. It was no accident, he thought. Someone killed both men. Someone who disappeared into the forest, leaving footprints behind. And he wasn't going to rest until he found who it was.

CHAPTER TWENTY-TWO

Esther Yoder shut the door behind her when the last of the three women gathered around her kitchen table.

"We need to be quick," she whispered as she sat down with them. "Jedediah will be home soon."

"At least pass the potatoes so we look as if we're busy cooking," one of the women said. Esther instantly reacted by bringing out a few spuds and knives, tossing them in the middle of the table.

Moments later there was a soft knock at the door and Lydia's head popped around.

"Sorry I'm late," she said. "With Rachel still missing I didn't get much sleep last night."

Esther pulled out a chair and gestured for her to sit down, popping a few potatoes on the table in front of her.

"What's this about, anyway?" Lydia asked as her eyes looked to the four women seated at the table.

"You invited *her*?" the most senior in the group asked, her face making it abundantly clear that Lydia wasn't welcome.

"She has every right to be here, Louise. This concerns her now too," Esther said.

"We don't know that," one of the other women uttered, her voice a near whisper.

"Except, I think we do know," Esther replied.

"Know what? What's happening here?" Lydia asked as she looked to Esther for answers.

Esther shuffled into a chair on the opposite side of the table, her eyes darting among the women's faces before landing on Lydia's.

"First, you have to give us your word that what we're about to tell you doesn't leave this room, okay Lydia?" Esther said as she leaned across the table.

Lydia's brows pulled into a frown.

When she didn't answer, the tone of Esther's voice was stern as she spoke again.

"Lydia, do you understand? You cannot breathe a word about this to anyone, least of all Samuel."

"But he's my husband. We don't keep secrets from each other and since when do we enter into gossiping? The *Ordnung* is very clear about—"

"Forget what the *Ordnung* says, Lydia," Louise cut her off. "I have been around long enough to tell you that there's nothing in the *Ordnung* that teaches us about any of this."

"And as our midwife, Louise should know," another woman who was the wife of one of the farriers said.

"I have no idea what's going on here, but this doesn't feel right," Lydia said as she moved her chair back and stood up.

Esther stood up too.

"Believe me, Lydia, none of what we're doing here feels right. But as your bishop's wife, I am telling you we didn't have any choice in the matter, and it is our belief that God approves of what we're doing here. Someone had to step in and do what the men in this community should have done a very long time ago. Trust me when I tell you that this is the only way so if you want your daughter safe and at home again, you'll sit back down and hear what we have to say."

The room was silent as the small group of women waited for Lydia to sit down. When she didn't, it was Louise who spoke her mind again.

"She's not ready, Esther. This was a bad idea to bring her in on this."

Esther's eyes didn't leave Lydia's face as she sat back down and folded her hands on top of the table in front of her, waiting for Lydia to take her seat again.

"What does any of this have to do with Rachel?" Lydia asked with a trembling voice, still standing.

"She's missing, is she not?" Esther asked.

Lydia dropped down into the chair, her body upright and tense as her eyes locked with Esther's.

"Where is she? What have you done with my Rachel?"

"What have *we* done?" the farrier's wife said with a trace of bitterness in her voice. "It's what we *haven't* done that's in question here, what we should have done years ago when we first realized what was going on. That's what you should be asking us instead." She dropped a half-peeled potato noisily on the table in front of her and crossed her arms over her chesty body.

"Okay, let's stay calm, ladies. We're not going to achieve anything by losing our tempers," Esther said.

"Will someone please tell me what's going on here? You're talking in riddles about Rachel, and I haven't the foggiest idea what you're talking about." Lydia's voice was raised.

"Hush!" Louise responded quickly. "Keep your voice down or you'll get all of us shunned."

Esther's hand reached across the table and took hold of Lydia's and saw her confused eyes were now flooded with tears as she looked back at her. Esther squeezed Lydia's hand as she answered her.

"We believe Rachel was taken advantage of by Dr. Fisher." Esther's voice was low and calm when she uttered the words.

Lydia snatched her hand from Esther's.

"That's absurd, not to mention ungodly. It's sinful to say the least. Why would you bring such shame upon my daughter?" She wiped away the tears from each cheek before she straightened her apron and nervously smoothed it out over her lap.

"I don't think you're understanding us, Lydia. Did you hear what Esther said?" Louise asked when Lydia didn't respond where she quietly sat staring at her hands on her lap.

"It's a mistake, you're making a mistake," Lydia eventually responded, her voice tinged with denial.

"We don't think so," Louise said. "Dr. Fisher had been treating her for months now, had he not?"

Lydia's body was tense, her fingers now fiddling in her lap in reaction to what the women were saying.

"She's not answering because she knows it's true," the farrier's wife said. "Don't you, Lydia? You knew what he was doing to Rachel, and you did nothing to stop it."

Lydia remained silent, her eyes fixed to her lap.

"That's because she was once a victim too, weren't you, Lydia?" Louise said softly.

A lonely tear dropped into Lydia's lap when she looked up into Louise's eyes without having to utter a single word to confirm her accusations.

Esther stood up and walked around the table, her arms wrapping around Lydia's shoulders as she stood behind her.

"It's okay, Lydia. You don't have to carry this around with you anymore. I was once in the exact place you find yourself in right now. The only difference is, you have all of us, something I wish I had back then. That's why we're here - to put a stop to this before another one of our girls goes missing."

Lydia wrestled herself loose from Esther's embrace and jumped up out of the chair. She drew a sudden breath, one hand covering her mouth.

"You killed Dr. Fisher! Murderers! Did you kill Brother Lapp too? I will not be a part of this evil! I will not!" Lydia yelled and raced from the kitchen, only to run straight into the bishop where he had just walked through the door.

CHAPTER TWENTY-THREE

Bishop Jedediah's hands closed over Lydia's arms as he grabbed hold of her when she lost her balance and nearly fell back onto the floor.

"What in heaven's name is this about?" he asked, looking at his wife, Esther, when she came rushing toward them.

Behind her, the women around the table scrambled to their feet.

"Esther, what's going on here?" the bishop asked again when Lydia pushed herself away and stormed out of the house.

"Nothing. She's just distraught over Rachel's disappearance, that's all," Esther half fibbed as the other women hurriedly excused themselves and left.

But it was evident that her husband did not believe a

word she said as he stopped her from rushing after the women.

"Don't make me order a shunning for lying to me, Esther Yoder," he said.

Esther swung around, her eyes narrow when she stared into her husband's eyes.

"I told you, Jed. Lydia's upset because her daughter is missing. It's what mothers do when their children go missing, or have you forgotten how it nearly killed me when Joanna disappeared?"

The bishop's face was hard; his jaw clenched as he fought back the urge to yell back at his wife's bitter words.

The room went still around them, each locked into silence as they wrestled with the memories of years gone by.

"Why didn't you tell the sheriff about Joanna, Jedediah? You should have told him," Esther said dejectedly.

"It's none of his business what happens inside this community. If I had my way, he and his men wouldn't even be here right now. We've always handled our affairs in a private manner, without the English getting involved. This is no different. Or is waywardness ruling your heart so much that you think I am not capable of governing my own community?"

Esther dropped down into the sofa chair next to her.

"That's not what I'm saying at all. But what if Rachel's disappearance is linked to Joanna's? Are you not in the least suspicious about any of this? What's so wrong with wanting to spare a mother's heart from having to go through what we did?"

Jedediah sat down in a nearby chair.

"I don't think this has any connection to our daughter's disappearance, Esther. The child was troubled. Her mind wasn't in a sound place. Besides, that was a long time ago."

"*The child* was our daughter, Jed! Our little girl, no older than Rachel is now. She was what the English call depressed, not crazy. We weren't there for her, our own daughter. Like we were ashamed of her for some absurd reason. We should have drawn closer to her, helped her, not shun her. It forced her to run away."

Hurt flickered across Jedediah's face as he looked at his wife.

"I am not to blame for our daughter leaving. We disciplined according to the *Ordnung*. She had free will and was old enough to do as she pleased."

"*You* were the one who disciplined her, Jed. I never agreed. You showed her no mercy or grace when you should have. We women are forced to go with whatever you men decide, even if it means losing our children. How is that just? Where's the compassion in that?"

"Are you doubting God's laws, Esther? It's how God created order and you shouldn't be questioning it, much less allow or encourage the women of this community to band together in such blatant disobedience against their husbands. What's gotten into you?"

Esther got to her feet.

"What's gotten into me? I should ask you the same question. You're the bishop. You should be doing more to find the Beilers' daughter. Instead, you're just sitting back and doing nothing, just like you did when Joanna went missing!"

She spat the words at her husband. Words that were fueled by rage, regret, and blame like pent-up venom that had been stored away for years.

"There are things in this community you know nothing about, Jedediah. Horrible, evil things and we will not sit by and let it happen anymore."

She turned to leave when he called her back.

"Don't make me punish you, Esther. You are acting out of God's order, and I will not tolerate this behavior, not from you or any of the women in this community."

Esther turned back to look at her husband, her eyes filled with fire.

"We have been silenced long enough and it stops here, whatever the consequences."

She opened the front door, looking back over her shoulder.

"I can't believe that you are so blinded by your conceited governance that you cannot see the evil that's right in front of your face, Jedediah."

When she turned to leave, Angus was standing on her doorstep, his eyes full of questions.

Dismay rippled through Esther's insides when she realized he had overheard her comment. For the briefest of moments, she just stood there, staring into the sheriff's eyes. Then, with one last stern look at her husband, she brushed past Angus and ran off.

Angus glimpsed the bishop's face, embarrassment front and center in his eyes where he stood silent in his doorway before shutting the door in Angus' face.

Angus turned and ran after Esther.

"Mrs. Yoder," he yelled after her as she disappeared between a row of houses.

When he was once again within earshot, he shouted her name again, but she kept walking, this time faster, her head concentrating on the ground in front of her.

"I just want to talk, Mrs. Yoder. I can help," he tried again.

His words made her slow down just enough for Angus to realize it had had an effect on her so he kept at it.

"If you let me, I can help. Please let me help."

She stopped, her head bowed and her hands folded across her waist.

"I'm sorry you had to see that, Sheriff."

Esther turned and started to walk away.

"What did you mean when you said there was evil your husband isn't seeing?"

His question brought her to a halt once again, her back still turned towards him.

"The world is full of evil. I was merely pointing it out to him."

"While that is very true, Mrs. Yoder, with respect, I

don't think that's what you meant when you said that to him. If there's something you're not telling me, now's the time. I can help you."

She remained silent, her back to him, her eyes looking straight ahead of her.

"Do you know where Rachel is? Do you know who killed Dr. Fisher, or Mr. Lapp?"

Esther finally turned around to face Angus, her eyes filled with contempt.

"Hopefully, both Dr. Fisher and Brother Lapp are burning in hell where they belong. As for Rachel, I don't know any more than you do. Now, if you will excuse me, I would like to be there for her mother while you do everything you can to bring her daughter home safe and sound."

When she turned and left, Angus let her go, but as he stood there between the quiet rural houses watching her walk away, he couldn't help but feel that beneath the tranquil Amish facade, the seemingly peaceful community was harboring a dreadful secret. And if his instincts weren't failing him, it had everything to do with Rachel's disappearance and the two corpses in his morgue.

CHAPTER TWENTY-FOUR

When Caleb sneaked away from the search party, he made sure no one saw him, least of all his angry father. The morning breeze cut into his cheeks as his feet carried his trembling body as fast as they could. Angus was right; he should put his hurt and anger to better use in searching for Rachel. She was all he had left.

Heading to where the bridge crossed over the river into the bordering land, his shoes crunched noisily in the soft snow with each step he took, leaving an undesired trail of footprints behind. But time was running out. They had to find Rachel before another sunset came around. Worrying about someone following him or his father's ridicule were the last things on his mind. All he cared about was making sure he found his sister first, before the sheriff arrested her for crimes he knew deep in his heart she didn't commit. He knew Rachel like no one else. She didn't have it in her to kill a fly. If he had to wager on it, she was likely to be hiding out somewhere instead.

Caleb decided he'd cross over into the neighboring property. The small pedestrian bridge was the only way to access the land and unless the search party knew about it, the piece of land would be the last place they'd go looking for her—at least for now.

He picked up the pace, traversing the icy ground with care. When he reached the foot of the bridge, he stopped briefly to survey the area around him. The property on the other side of the river was covered with dense trees, the ground beneath blanketed in uneven patches of snow and dead foliage. He had only been there once with a few of his friends and very nearly got lost between the tall trees. Had it not been for one of them remembering the way out, they may have never made it back alive. Perhaps that's what had happened to Rachel. Perhaps she just lost her way and couldn't get out.

He held onto the thought of finding her alive, hunkered down somewhere in the hollow of a tree, cold and afraid. His heart skipped several beats as urgency rushed through his body. As he crossed the river, the wooden bridge groaned under his weight. His eyes searched desperately between the shadowy foliage as soon as he stepped onto the property on the other side. There was no stopping him now and he rushed in between the trees, zigzagging through the forest as fast as his legs would carry him. When the tall trees closed around him and he could no longer see the river or the bridge behind him, fear teased at his stomach. But there was no turning back now.

"Rachel," he whisper-called. "It's me, Caleb." He stopped and listened for her voice, even just a moan was all he needed to hear.

"Rachel," he called again then repeated her name three more times, but there was no sound returning apart from the whooshing breeze that moved through the treetops high above his head. Again he called, changing direction every few paces so the wind would carry his voice. When he briefly lost his bearings, he realized that it would have been nearly impossible for Rachel to find her way out, especially in the dark.

Fear no longer teased him. Instead, it had settled into a heavy lump inside his stomach. Brief moments of panic washed over him as he tried to make sense of his position. Forced to stop and turn in all directions to find his way again, he lingered between the dense trees. Desperate to take control of his spiraling angst, he closed his eyes and inhaled deeply through his nose to calm himself down. His eyes flashed open, certain he smelled smoke. With his senses on high alert, he sniffed the air again, spinning around in the hope of identifying from where the smoke was coming. He had entirely lost his bearings and had been wandering deeper into the forest so knew he was too far away from the community for the smoke to come from there. Perhaps he was close to a hunter's cabin, he thought, but ruled that prospect out too. The land was private and belonged to the Amish and had not ever been inhabited. His final hypothesis was the most probable. If Rachel was lost in the forest, she'd have made a fire to stay warm. Excitement burst into his stomach.

"Rachel!" he shouted louder, his body still stuck in one spot as he spun around in search of the source of the smoke.

But still there was no reply.

To his right the ground stretched into a steady downward slope and without giving it another thought, he ran in that direction. Beneath his feet the rotten leaves were slippery with a thin layer of snow, causing him to slip and fall several times. Steadying his feet as he made his way down the slope to the shadowy valley between the dense trees, there was no stopping him now, his racing pulse being his only guideline. As he neared the foot of the hill, the smell of woodsmoke became stronger and excitement entangled with dread quickened his pulse even more. When he reached the bottom, he stopped to take in his surroundings. From somewhere between the trees in front of him a branch broke and leaves shuffled.

"Rachel!" he yelled out without thinking, instantly regretting it when another sound came from the opposite direction. This time his instincts told him it wasn't his sister.

Panic raised the hair at the back of his neck, his spine now straight as his body reacted to the environment that had suddenly turned strangely eerie. He held back, as if his body detected danger his eyes hadn't yet seen. Deciding to err on the side of caution, he took cover behind a large trunk, his eyes darting wildly between the trees where he thought he'd heard the noises. From the corner of his eye, he could have sworn he spotted movement, yet there was no sound. A deer perhaps, he thought. Squinting his eyes and craning his neck to better see into the shadows, he focused his sights on the spot behind a tree. Not seeing anything from that angle, he swung his body around the other side of the tree, peering and stretching to better see deep into the forest. Moments later, an arrow whizzed inches past his face and lodged into the tree's thick trunk right beside him.

CHAPTER TWENTY-FIVE

Horror ripped through Caleb, his eyes held prisoner by the threatening arrow that wobbled in the trunk directly beside him. He no longer felt the cold that had pushed up into his legs, nor the sharp, rough edges of the bark that pushed into his frozen hands. Shock had numbed every muscle in his body. His emotions ran wild with him, thudding inside his chest like a trapped animal trying to kick his way out of a predator's vice. Not knowing how to escape the danger, he pushed his back into the tree, leaning his head against the hard edges while wishing it would just swallow him whole. Shutting his eyes, he swallowed hard to rid his throat of the dry spot that had taken up space there. Then he waited, listening for the forest sounds that he hoped would give his hunter's position away. But they didn't; the forest had gone deadly quiet around him.

When he finally plucked up the courage to look out from behind the tree, his eyes settled on the arrow next to his face. It was like nothing he had ever seen before, almost primitive in nature. At first he thought he'd pull it out, use it as a weapon, but then another sound echoed from the forest behind him. This time it was closer.

He fell back against the tree, his legs felt heavy and glued to the forest floor. There was nowhere to run, nowhere to hide. Whoever was trying to kill him knew those woods far better than he did. Dread washed over his body. What if they had done this to Rachel? What if she too was hunted and couldn't get away? What if she was left for dead?

Refusing to accept the latter premise, he pushed the grim thought out of his mind and told himself to stay focused. His eyes briefly darted back to the arrow in the tree next to him. It came close to hitting him, too close, but staying there, hiding like a coward wouldn't help him find his sister. He would do anything to save her, even if it cost him his life.

Rachel was in grave danger, now more than ever before, and she needed him.

Needing no more convincing, Caleb decided he'd try to outrun his hunter and find his way back to get help instead. Once Rachel was safe and out of danger, he'd hire the best lawyers to defend her if that's what it took.

He cautiously peered around the tree, keeping a sharp eye out for the archer. When he thought he was safe, he tried running for cover behind an even larger tree, but another arrow smashed into the ground right next to his feet. For a microsecond, he thought his heart was going to stop but adrenaline pushed into his veins and allowed him to make another attempt to escape. This time, he ran in a different direction. But no matter how hard he tried to remain in control of his legs, fear turned them to a wobbly mess that made him trip over his feet several times before he fell, knocking the wind from his lungs. *Get up, get up*, he heard a little voice shout inside his head. Scrambling on all fours across the forest floor, he was able to push himself up and dove to take cover behind another tree. His raging heartbeat sent his entire body into overdrive, and he spared no time before he made another attempt at running to the next tree.

But no sooner did he succeed at getting behind a tree when another arrow whooshed past, the air teasing his cheek as it sped past. This time the near killing was enough to firmly jolt his legs into action and he sprinted past a number of trees without stopping. Panting, his heartbeat running wild inside his chest, he kept running, bounding from trunk to trunk in an effort to escape whoever was trying his utmost to kill him. All he could do was run, as fast as his legs and the unsteady ground would allow. Never once did he stop. Never once did he care to look back. All he did was run, farther and farther in the opposite direction until his body felt weak, but still he dared not stop.

Another arrow zipped toward him, this time ripping into the denim fabric that covered his knee. A deep groan escaped from the back of his throat, echoing through the quiet forest. Caleb fell to the ground mid-sprint, nearly knocking all his breath out. He skidded across the snowy sludge and came to a sudden stop when he smashed into the base of a large tree. Several more low groans told him he likely bruised a few ribs. He was alive at least. When he finally caught his breath again, he peeled his body from the ground, turned on his side, and pushed himself along with one leg, dragging his body using his elbows until he was sitting upright behind the tree. The flesh on the side of his knee burned like a blazing fire. He closed his hands over the ripped fabric, not stopping to assess the extent of his injury. All he could focus on was staying alive long enough to find help and to find Rachel.

He tried to get up, but it wasn't as easy as he had hoped and he fell back against the tree, his injured leg barely able to take the full weight of his body. A strange numbing sensation pushed into his knee. Caleb rested his head against the tree. It felt like the arrow was still stuck in his leg but he checked again and saw that it wasn't. There was no time to inspect the wound and he pushed harder to get up. This time he succeeded, barely. Leaning against the tree trunk, he rubbed his eyes with the base of his palm, desperate to rid his eyes from the sudden blurry vision. He must have knocked his head during the fall, he thought.

When he felt steady enough to make a run for it, he searched for a way out, listening for his attacker's whereabouts to help him. A short distance behind him, twigs snapped, and he knew his attacker must be closing in on him. His heart skipped a beat; his eyes frantically searched in all directions. It was as if the entire forest had turned against him; his senses ran wild with the sounds around him. Panic ripped through his body. Even if he succeeded at getting a head start, running fast enough to get away would be nearly impossible in his current condition. He shifted some weight onto his leg to test his ability, expecting to be hit by pangs of pain. Except what stopped him from running was that he had hardly any feeling in it at all.

His head went into a tailspin, flooding fear into his every cell. Unable to hold himself upright a moment longer, Caleb slumped back and fell to the ground.

CHAPTER TWENTY-SIX

Lydia stormed into her house to find her husband perched on the edge of the couch, his head in his hands. Panic ripped through her insides.

"What's happened?" she asked, frozen in place. "Is it Rachel? Have they found her? Where is she? Is she okay?" She fired a barrage of questions at him.

When he lifted his head to look at his wife, his eyes were red, evidence that he had been crying.

Lydia's insides turned upside down as she crossed the floor toward him.

"Samuel, where's Rachel? What's going on?"

"They're still out looking for her," Samuel finally answered dejectedly.

The tension in Lydia's stomach lessened and she took a seat next to him on the couch, curling one arm around his shoulders.

"Why have you been crying then? We can't lose hope now. We have to keep praying that God will bring her back to us."

Samuel tilted his head to one side, a troubled look in his eyes.

"What have we done to deserve this lot, Lydia? All my life I've striven to be a good man, a good father. Like Amos in the Bible - an upstanding member of this community, serving under God's law. Why would He take our child from us, punish us like this?"

He hung his head forward again, fresh tears dripping onto the floor and his shoes.

"You mustn't talk like this, Samuel. She's not dead."

Lydia got up and walked into the kitchen, emerging shortly after with two mugs of coffee. Handing one to Samuel, she said, "Here, drink up. You need to stop wallowing in your self-pity and get out there and help Caleb find our daughter instead."

Samuel's eyes were wild when they met his wife's.

"I would rather die a thousand deaths than be near that traitor."

He plunked the mug on the table in front of them, spilling half the contents onto his hand and table as he stood up.

"Samuel!" Lydia said as the horror of his words overwhelmed her. "You cannot mean that."

"Oh, but I do, Lydia, and you will never speak of him

or mention his name again. Never! The son we once had, is dead to me - to us - you hear me?"

He stormed to where his coat draped over the coatrack behind the front door. Lydia rose to her feet, a despondent look on her face.

"Why are you saying that? Caleb is our son, our only son."

"It's because of him that our Rachel is gone! He's to blame. Were you aware that they've been in contact with each other all these years, behind our backs? They wrote letters to each other, smuggled them in and out of here like thieves. That man has no respect for our faith or the *Ordnung*. He polluted our little girl; he filled her head with all sorts of evil. That's why she ran away, because of Caleb!"

Lydia covered her mouth with one hand as the other one clutched at her stomach.

"No, I don't believe that. Rachel would never do that. You're wrong, Samuel, you're wrong!"

She dropped onto the couch and buried her face in her hands as she sobbed.

"There's no mistake, Lydia. I saw one of the letters myself and heard him admit it to the person in charge of the search party. It was one of those beautiful pieces of lavender parchments she always crafted, and it had her hand lettering on the front."

Samuel slipped his coat on and reached for his scarf,

his heart bitter with hatred as Lydia tried to reason with him.

"You're not thinking clearly. You're distraught over Rachel; that's understandable. I am too. But Caleb is still our son, Samuel, and Rachel is our daughter. I gave birth to both of them because that's how God willed it. Bitterness is blinding you, turning your heart to ice, and all because our children have inquiring minds. What's wrong with that? Didn't God create them with that very inquisitiveness? Who are we to stop them from using their gifts, their free will that our graceful Father has given them?"

"Stop, just stop!" Samuel barked, his lips pressed together in a thin line. "It is not your place to speak against my wishes, against my better judgement. Your place as a woman is to tend to the house and the child we have left. It is not your right to question my rules and it is certainly not your place to teach the Lord's scriptures."

Lydia's anger seethed as she watched him turn around and reach for the door handle. Bile pushed up from her stomach and into her throat, forcing its way out in the way of words she could no longer hold back.

"No! I will not be quiet not anymore, Samuel Beiler. I've had to live with it all bottled up inside of me for years and years and I will not be silenced anymore!"

She stormed towards the exit, pushing her husband out of the way as she yanked the door open.

"You are out of line, Lydia!" Samuel yelled after her as she stepped outside. "Come back here, right now!"

Lydia felt her blood boil with anger with her husband's words and she spun around to face him, closing the distance between them and stopping inches away from her husband's face.

"Dr. Fisher deserved to die. Jonathan Lapp too, as do half a dozen other men in this community. They're all evil, Samuel, possessed by Satan himself, and I will no longer bite my tongue in fear of being shunned because of what Dr. Fisher did to me and countless other young girls and women in this community. We will not be silenced any longer. You want to talk about duty? You men are supposed to protect your wives and daughters, but you haven't been doing that at all. Instead, you've allowed evil to fester under a blanket of perfection. You turn the other way, sweep it under the rug, and bind us by silence and submissiveness until there's no out apart from running away. If anyone is to blame for Rachel's leaving, it's you and the rest of the spineless men who live here."

As Lydia spat the words at her husband, years of pent-up shame, fury, and fear exploded into her cells. It was as if the walls of her heart had burst open and she was unable to stop her emotions from gushing out. Like steam propelling a train, her legs compelled her to turn and run.

Lydia Beiler hurried off to Esther's house, resolute to join the other women and partake in whatever it was they were doing to find Rachel. She felt exhilarated, free. And freedom never tasted better.

CHAPTER TWENTY-SEVEN

Angus shut the door of the Lapp's house behind him and stood staring at the small herd of cows in the field across from him. He had hoped his interview with Jonathan Lapp's widow would yield something significant, anything that might indicate why anyone would want to kill him or the doctor. Except it didn't. He had nothing. No motive and no suspects, except Murphy's theory of the killer being an exotic Amazonian amphibian.

He rubbed at the knot of tension that had formed in his shoulder. It had been thirty-six hours since the first killing, a little less since Rachel's disappearance, another dead body in the short time since then, and no other clues. Word had already spread to the surrounding smaller towns and the *Weyport Herald* was hounding him for answers. Time wasn't on his side.

He walked closer to the cow pen and leaned his arms

on top of the wooden fence. "Lord," he whispered, "I really need your guidance here. Show me which direction to take. Help me find Rachel and whoever is responsible for these murders."

He lingered for a moment while watching the cattle, waiting to hear from God. But God was silent.

He took out his mobile phone and dialed the number for his office.

"Morning, Sheriff," Tammy answered in her usual cheerful manner. "How's the investigation going?"

"I'm afraid it's not going at all. That's why I'm calling."

"What do you need, how can I help?"

"I need you to have forensics run a DNA test on the head covering they found in the forest, confirm if it does in fact belong to Rachel Beiler, and I need it done yesterday."

"On it, Sheriff, anything else?"

"Yeah, is Miguel still held up with the union dispute at the docks? I could use his help over here."

"He is, and things are getting a bit heated over there. He's got his hands full trying to keep them from going at each other's throats. Tensions are running at an all-time high and with it being so close to Christmas, I'm not sure things will ease up for them to get what they want anytime soon. The fishery company is playing hardball and, if you ask me, they're using the Christmas season to their full advantage, if you know what I mean. I'm guessing they're intentionally avoiding responding in a timely fashion to buy them more time. I think they're hoping the fishermen will give in and let it go."

"I see. I guess at least on the bright side, the dispute is keeping the *Herald* off my back for a little while longer. I need all the time I can get right now."

"Yeah, since you brought it up, I've been keeping a lid on things, but we might need to put out a statement very soon, Sheriff. People are talking and the latest gossip is that there's a serial killer on the loose."

"Let's hope that's not the case but I hear you. I'll put something together and send you an email to forward onto the *Herald* as soon as I can. In the meantime, I need the DNA confirmation, and if you could dig a little deeper into Dr. Fisher's background for me, I'd appreciate that too."

"I'll call you as soon as I have something for you."

When they ended the call, Angus was determined to bring whatever secrets lingered behind the seemingly calm community's exterior to the surface. If there was the slightest chance that Rachel's disappearance was unrelated and that she had nothing to do with the murders, then it was plausible to assume she might have been abducted for knowing who the killer is or that she ran away to hide from him. Someone was responsible for these crimes if it wasn't Rachel, then the killer was still around somewhere, right in front of his nose. He was missing something and if it meant he needed to go back to the basics to crack the case, then that was precisely what needed to be done.

Deciding to have another conversation with Rachel's parents, he turned around and made his way back to the Beilers' house. He was experienced enough to know that young girls didn't just run away from home. They were her parents, after all, and that meant they probably knew more than they were letting on. Perhaps they had already found her and kept her hidden away somewhere, to protect her either from the law or from being killed by the real culprit. Either way, his gut told him that they were not telling all.

Neither Samuel nor Lydia Beiler was home when Angus got to their house. He turned and scanned the area.

One of his deputies was talking to a member of the community nearby, his black notebook in his hand. When the deputy spotted Angus, he abruptly paused his questioning and hurried over to meet him.

"Anything come up yet?" Angus asked the deputy as soon as he got to him.

"Nothing, Sheriff. They're all saying the same thing. What a good man Mr. Lapp was; how dedicated he was to serving the community, that type of thing. I've pretty much interviewed everyone and not one of them had anything bad to say about the man."

"What about the girl, Rachel? Have you spoken to her friends at all?"

The deputy nodded then flipped through his notepad.

"I have. No one knows anything. It seems the girl mostly kept to herself, or they're just not sharing. But one of her cousins said he last saw her when she came rushing out of the doctor's office. James is his name. He was the one who took the women into the little town to get supplies and deliver Rachel to her appointment with the first victim. So far, it looks as if he might have been one of the last two people who saw her before she went missing. Her mother, of course, being the only other person. Lydia Beiler and his mother are sisters."

"Good. Did he say if he noticed anything off with Rachel?"

The deputy shook his head.

"I didn't think to ask, Sheriff, sorry. He gave me the impression that he wasn't all that close to her so I doubt he would've noticed if something was off."

"I'd rather not assume anything at this point. It might be worth digging a little deeper. Any idea where I might find him?"

The deputy pointed at a shed a short distance away.

"He should be in there, where all the horse buggies are. He does the maintenance on them, like a buggy mechanic, if you know what I mean."

"Thanks. On another note, do you perhaps know where the Beilers are?"

The deputy's eyebrows pulled up, an amused look in his eyes as a smile took shape on his mouth.

"Yeah, that was quite a show. The two had an argument not that long ago, right there on their doorstep. It looked like Mrs. Beiler gave her husband a piece of her mind then hurried off and disappeared between the houses. Shortly after, Mr. Beiler rounded up a few of his men and they took off to the forest."

"Interesting. Any idea what they were arguing about?"

The deputy shrugged his shoulders.

"No idea, Sheriff, sorry, they spoke Amish. I just know that they were both pretty upset. He looked like he had been crying and Mrs. Beiler's voice was raised. I know from experience that when a woman's tone sounds like that, the husband usually ends up sleeping on the couch that night." He winked and shrugged his shoulders. "Then again, I could be entirely off the mark and it's just this thing with their daughter that's taking a toll on them."

"It's likely, although one can never assume anything when you're working a case. Whatever they argued about, I'll circle back to that later. I'm going to see what I can get out of James. In the meantime, keep at it with Rachel's friends. Someone here must know more than they're letting on."

The deputy nodded then promptly returned to continue gathering information from the man whom he had been questioning earlier.

CHAPTER TWENTY-EIGHT

When Angus left his deputy and made his way toward the buggy shed, he found a teenage boy who looked to be about fifteen years old, sitting on a stool hammering away at the wheel of one of the buggies.

"I'm looking for James," Angus said as he walked up to him.

"That'll be me," the teen answered as he stood up wiping his hands on his pants.

"I was wondering if I could ask you a few questions about Rachel and the last time you saw her."

James looked down at his feet.

"I should be out there helping them look for her, I know. But my parents said it is better that I stay out of it. I heard they found her bonnet, though."

"We don't know for sure if it is Rachel's yet."

"Yeah, but I heard the dogs found it so then it must be hers. Do you think she's dead?"

Angus chose not to answer the perceptive teenager's question.

"Tell me about when you last saw her. I understand you drove her to her appointment with Dr. Fisher."

A slight frown twitched on James' face.

"She didn't do it, Sheriff. There's no way. Rachel has one of the purest hearts I know."

"I believe you, James. I'm running through a list of questions, that's all."

"Yeah, but everyone's thinking she did it though. They can't say it out loud because it'll get them a shunning."

"Well, in my line of work you are innocent until proven guilty. So, how about it? Will you help me prove her innocence by answering my questions?"

The teen nodded slowly.

"Do you know how long her doctor's appointment lasted?"

James seemed hesitant to answer, as if he was first trying to find the right words.

"I'm just trying to establish if there might have been a reason for her to want to run away," Angus pushed a little harder.

"Well, I'm sure it's nothing but I did think it strange at the time," James answered.

"Go on."

"Usually, her appointments were about thirty minutes

or so but this time she went in and came straight out again. I asked her about it, but she didn't say anything. It was as if she was in a hurry or something. She just ran across the road to find our mothers."

"You're doing good, James. Did you notice anything strange about her when she left the doctor?"

James' face turned somber.

"I don't want Rachel to get into any trouble, but she's not been acting the same since she started her fixings with the doctor. I think she was scared of him."

"What about the ride home? Did she say anything to you then? Did she seem upset at all?"

He shook his head then answered.

"She didn't say a single word all the way home. But that's how it's been for a while now whenever we came back home after she'd been to see the doctor. Come to think of it, she was fine every other time we went in for supplies but not when she had to see him. I reckoned it was just woman stuff, you know."

"Woman stuff?"

"Yeah, you know," James blushed, looking away. "They only see him when they're getting ready for marriage or when they're about to have babies."

"I see. Do you know of anyone else who had been seeing the doctor recently?"

James scratched his head.

"They all go as soon as they turn sixteen. Ask any of the girls."

Angus grew quiet before he asked his next question.

"What about the men, do they go too?"

James shook his head, a wry smile pushing a blush into his cheeks.

"No way, only the women go. Like I said, it's woman stuff."

His answer left an unsettled feeling in the pit of Angus' stomach, one that made him sick with the suspicion that now flooded his mind. And it definitely needed more clarification.

"So let me get this straight, James. Are you saying that the doctor only treated the women, never any men, ever?"

James cocked his head to one side.

"Pretty much, yes. I never actually realized it until now but yes, I think so. There were a few of the senior men who went sometimes but not that many. Like Mr. Lapp, for example, he was one of his regulars. God bless his soul."

Angus frowned.

"Mr. Lapp? You're saying he was a regular patient of Dr. Fisher's."

James nodded.

"Who else? Can you give me names of any other men who also saw the doctor?"

The teen thought for a moment.

"Not really, although I do remember one of the elders went once or twice but that was a while ago. Back when Joanna disappeared."

Angus felt as if he had been punched in the gut.

"Joanna? What do you mean? Who's Joanna?" he asked.

"Sorry, I thought you knew. I shouldn't have said anything." James turned away and busied himself with the buggy's wheel.

"James, I'm not here to get you into any kind of trouble so I give you my word this will stay between us, but it's important that you tell me everything you know. Rachel is still out there somewhere and we're running out of time. Who is Joanna and what happened to her?"

James turned back to him, a reticent look on his face.

"Joanna was the bishop's daughter. She disappeared quite a few years ago. Just vanished in thin air. Much like Rachel, come to think of it. They found her bloody clothes, torn to shreds in the woods. Bishop Yoder said she was killed by a black bear. It nearly broke Ms. Esther's heart. She was their only child."

Angus struggled to control his heart that thumped with intensity inside his chest.

"Do you remember how old Joanna was when she disappeared?"

James took a moment to think.

"About my age if I remember correctly. I was very young at the time, maybe ten, I think. Yeah, that feels about right. She was already sixteen. I remember now because Caleb had just celebrated his eighteenth birthday and the two of them were supposed to get married that year."

Angus could hardly believe his ears.

"Caleb? As in Rachel's brother? That Caleb?"

"Uh-huh, the two of them were in love."

"Is that why Caleb left the community?"

James shrugged one shoulder.

"Probably, I mean the two of them had a huge argument just before she ran away. Rachel told me."

"A fight? Do you know what it was about?"

"Not really. The adults don't really tell us kids much about these things, but whatever it was about also upset Caleb's father, Mr. Beiler."

"Why do you say that?"

"Because after they couldn't find Joanna, Caleb had words with his father and not long after that, Caleb also left."

"And you say they never found her?"

James nodded his head.

"What makes you think she ran away?"

"Because she took a bag of clothes with her. If something bad happened to her she wouldn't have packed a bag, right?"

Angus agreed, nodding in response.

"You've been very helpful, James. Thank you."

Angus walked away, his mind racing with the new information. His investigation had just taken a turn in a different direction.

CHAPTER TWENTY-NINE

Lydia's heart pounded inside her chest as she wound her way between the houses. With her head held down, her eyes pinned to the ground as if she was hiding her face, she moved faster toward Esther's house. In all the years she had been married to Samuel, she had never dared speak to him with such anger and such contempt. She'd been a good wife; loyal, submissive, and reverent of his standing in the community and their home. But something deep inside her had snapped and she no longer had the restraint to hold back. She'd lost too much.

Shame washed into her heart with every step she took. Perhaps the Holy Spirit was revealing the way she had sinned toward her husband and God, she thought. She forced the guilt aside, feeling no regret for her outburst, no desire to ask Samuel for his forgiveness, and no inclination to turn back and pretend that nothing was wrong. Because nothing had been right for far too long. Keeping silent had been her only vice, holding her hostage for the longest time. That's what she regretted most. For not speaking up back then, for not doing something about it all those years ago. For not choosing her children over her husband. If she had, perhaps her sweet Rachel would be home, and her only son wouldn't have left.

Tears filled her eyes as heartache poured through her chest. There was no turning back now. Nor did she want to. This was her chance, her only chance to fix what had been broken for far too long. For the sake of her children, for the sake of her freedom, to no longer be held captive by the despicable things that happened to her and Rachel.

New found courage spilled into her heart and propelled her into a slow jog. She rounded the last corner and burst into Esther's house without stopping to knock. When she stumbled in through the front door, she found Esther alone in her kitchen.

"Lydia! What's the matter?" Esther reacted to her abrupt entrance, dropping the ladle noisily into the pot of soup she was cooking.

But Lydia didn't have to utter a single word. Her eyes told Esther exactly why she was there.

Moving the pot hastily to one side of the stove, Esther pulled Lydia into one of the chairs at her kitchen table.

"You're doing the right thing, Lydia. I know it might not feel like it right now, but when you have Rachel home safe and sound you'll be glad you did it."

Lydia wiped away the tears that were now spilling down her cheeks as she looked full into Esther's face.

"I should have spoken up a long time ago, Esther. I only pray that God can forgive me for the part I played in it all, and for sinning against my husband."

Esther's hands closed firmly around Lydia's arms.

"It wasn't your fault, Lydia, none of it was. What Dr. Fisher did to you, to all of us was wrong and it was his sin. His and the other men that behaved alike. And God will punish them for it. He has already."

Lydia's eyes were full of questions, her heart yearning to ask her friend if she and the other women killed Dr. Fisher and Brother Lapp, but she held back, fearing she'd offend her, fearing the truth.

Esther shifted in the chair next to her, her voice low and steady as she spoke.

"Does Samuel know you're here, what you're doing?"

Lydia quickly shook her head.

"No, and I won't tell him either."

"Good, you're doing the right thing, trust me."

Lydia watched as Esther jumped to her feet, cast a quick glance toward the front door, shut the kitchen door, then knelt in front of her pantry cupboard. From the bottom shelf she lifted out a large basket of onions and plunked it on the floor next to her before she stuck her hand back inside the dark cavity and pulled out a small wooden box. When she got up, she turned around and placed the box on the table in front of her, lifting the lid to reveal a two-way radio.

Lydia's mouth dropped open.

"Where did you get that?" she whispered, her eyes wide.

"We're borrowing it, that's all."

"You mean you stole it from the search and rescue team. Oh, we're going to go to hell for this, Esther," Lydia said, angst written all over her face.

"I'll take my chances," Esther replied as she switched the radio on and spoke into it.

"Nightingale, come in, over," she said, repeating the call twice.

Louise's voice came back over the radio.

"Receiving you loud and clear, Phoenix."

"Get the others. Rendezvous, five minutes, over."

"Copy that, Phoenix. Over and out."

Esther tucked the radio into her apron pocket before spinning around to return the onions to the pantry.

"What on earth was all that?" Lydia said as she watched Esther hide the empty wooden box behind the basket of vegetables.

When Esther turned to face her, she had a mischievous smile on her face.

"Just a bunch of bored old women having a bit of fun to lighten the mood, is all." She winked. "Now come, we don't have a lot of time."

Esther rushed ahead toward the door, Lydia close behind her.

With her hand resting on the doorknob, Esther turned to Lydia.

"I suggest you leave that panicked look on your face behind. We don't need to draw any attention to ourselves now. We're just two friends out for a walk, got it?"

Lydia nodded, desperate to control the tension that had knotted in her stomach.

Esther led the way, quickly walking toward a row of houses on the far side of the property. As she caught up and walked next to Esther, zigzagging between the houses, Lydia did as Esther instructed and held her composure, even managing to greet a couple they passed along the way.

"Where are we going?" Lydia whispered after they turned another corner.

"Almost there," Esther whispered back.

A few short moments later, they stopped outside a house Lydia hadn't been to before, her nerves suddenly taut with fear of the unknown.

"Whose house is this?" she asked as a horse neighed nearby.

But Esther didn't answer. Instead, she glanced in all directions to see if anyone was around then knocked on the door three times. Within seconds, the farrier's wife yanked it open and quickly ushered them inside.

Once inside, the farrier's wife cast a cautious look at Esther.

"She's fine," Esther answered quickly. "Lydia has decided to join us."

Esther flashed Lydia an assuring smile before she followed the farrier's wife through the house and into a room in the back where Louise, the midwife, and several other women sat around a quilting table.

CHAPTER THIRTY

"Good, you're all here," Esther said as she ushered Lydia to one of the nearby chairs.

Lydia smiled nervously at the half a dozen women who now stared at her. Some with sympathy in their eyes, others with suspicion. She recognized a few of them from church, others she had hardly spoken to. They ranged in age - the oldest being Louise, the midwife, the youngest, around twenty or so.

"Lydia," Esther said, startling her. "Every single one of these women has faced the same trauma you have. Two of them sadly lost their daughters. One tragically took her own life, and the other girl ran away. Just like Rachel did... and Joanna."

Her voice cracked as she said her daughter's name out loud then briefly looked down to gather herself again.

"We have all fallen victim to Dr. Fisher's sin, you included."

Lydia found herself blushing as Esther spoke aloud the truth she'd been hiding for so long.

"But," Esther continued, "unfortunately Dr. Fisher wasn't the only sinner among the men in this community. We believe there are several men currently living in our community whose flesh has ruled their hearts for quite some time now. Brother Lapp was one of them."

A few of the women shuffled uncomfortably in their chairs as Esther continued.

"For years we have been told not to speak of these things, to turn the other cheek, even to pray for them, but no more. The truth cannot be swept under the rug any longer. Rachel's leaving showed us that we women must take matters into our own hands. We need to stand up for ourselves, do what the honorable men should have done but were too cowardly to act. The time is now, Lydia. There is no more denying it or pretending that we're okay with it because we're not. Our bodies are sacred, temples of our Lord most high, and no man has the right to take what isn't his."

Two women affirmed Esther's statement with a loud "Amen" before Esther continued.

"The women you see here today have formed a pact among us to expose these evil men, to stop them from hurting us, our sisters, our daughters."

Lydia's palms were clammy as Esther's words hit home.

"So, Lydia," Esther paused, her eyes never leaving Lydia's. "Are you sure you have the courage to fight the good fight alongside us? It won't be easy and it will challenge your boundaries and faith, but we believe it's what we have to do to put an end to the evil that has festered inside our community for much too long."

"But how?" Lydia heard herself ask, the courage she had summoned earlier fading. "How are we supposed to stop it if our husbands won't even listen to us? I told Samuel years ago when it happened to me, back when we were trying so hard to have another baby, but he refused to believe me. And when Rachel went missing, I tried to tell him again, but he lost all self-control and forbade me to ever speak of such evil again. How are we supposed to stop these men?"

Her questions were met with silence and sideways glances from the women. Lydia gasped, her hands covering her mouth as she read the room.

"You did kill them, didn't you? That's how you're stopping these men, by murdering them!"

Tears welled up in her eyes as she spoke the accusatory words, her hands still covering her mouth as if to stop more words from coming out. She waited for Esther to answer, to explain, to tell her it wasn't true. But Esther's eyes darted between the women whose gazes were fixed on Lydia's anguished face.

"Not exactly," Esther finally answered, her mouth and nose twisted to one side.

"Not exactly? What does that mean?" Lydia demanded.

"We think that there's someone else who must know about these men. Someone who isn't in our circle."

"Someone else, you mean the murderer?" Lydia guessed to which Esther nodded.

Lydia was on her feet now, pacing the small space around the circle of women.

"I don't understand. What is all this about then?" she asked, desperate for it to all make sense.

Louise spoke next.

"All we want to do is stop the sheriff from finding out who this person is. Throw him off the trail so to speak."

Lydia stopped.

"Have you lost your minds? You're sabotaging the investigation. There's a law against that among the English, you know. Not to mention that you're helping a cold-blooded killer get away with murder!"

Esther stood behind Lydia, her steady hands wrapped around Lydia's shoulders in an attempt to usher her back into her chair.

"I did warn you that your beliefs would be challenged, Lydia, but try to keep an open mind. We don't believe we're committing any evil here, merely buying time."

Disgust flushed into Lydia's face.

"Are you listening to yourself, Esther? You're the bishop's wife! You of all people should know that helping a murderer is no different from committing murder yourself."

"We don't know for sure that there is a murderer, Lydia," Louise spoke up again. "As far as we understand, they have no idea how Brother Lapp or Dr. Fisher died. For all we know, God struck them dead for what they've done. But what we do know is that the sheriff suspects Rachel."

"Rachel? There has to be a mistake," Lydia exclaimed as she sank back into her chair.

"I heard it with my own ears. It's true," one of the women added.

"Me too," said another.

"But...she couldn't have. Rachel could never be capable of doing such an evil thing."

Doubt crept into Lydia's heart as she recalled the time she was victimized by the doctor and temptation nearly got the better of her.

Esther's voice was gentle when she knelt next to her.

"We think Rachel ran away because it was her. She was the last to see the doctor alive, Lydia, and we think it was her footprints that the sheriff found in the snow behind Brother Lapp's barn. But, if we help Rachel finish what she started, we will also put a stop to the evil that has plagued this community for far too long."

As Esther's final attempt at persuasion washed over Lydia, the bitter sting of betrayal arrested her heart. When

Lydia looked Esther full in her face, her voice was calm and solid with conviction.

"My daughter is not capable of doing these despicable things you are accusing her of, and I will not sit here and listen to all of you telling me otherwise."

She got to her feet and turned to leave.

"If you turn your back on this, Lydia, you are no different from these men who put us in this predicament in the first place," Louise spat at her.

"Don't do this, Lydia," Esther added. "This is our chance to rid this community of the festering evil that had claimed the innocence of our daughters, of us. You cannot in good conscience let them get away with it any longer. We won't let you."

Esther's threat horrified Lydia as she opened the door to leave. With her heart and emotions in turmoil, fear pushed into her veins and she did the only thing her instincts told her to do. She ran.

CHAPTER THIRTY-ONE

Lydia's feet pounded the unpaved paths that wound between the houses. Behind her, Esther yelled after her to stop. She dared not turn around, dared not stop. Inside her chest, her heart beat hard and fast. Raw emotion and fear pulsed through her entire body. She tried desperately to control her tears but when she turned the final corner toward her house, they spilled over and ran down her cheeks. The door to her house came into view and she focused on it, pushing her legs to go faster. Noticing nothing else, she kept going. It wasn't until she slammed into someone that she was forced to stop. The impact nearly caused her to fall. When she looked up, she saw the sheriff, his curious eyes taking in the angst and tears on her face. Panic ripped through her, desperate to break free from his grip that had stopped her from falling onto the ground.

"Mrs. Beiler, it's me, Sheriff Reid. Is everything all right?"

Lydia glanced back at the path between the houses and saw Esther and Louise where they had stopped and stood watching from the shadows.

"Mrs. Beiler, is anything the matter? Did something happen?" Angus asked again as he steadied her on her feet.

Lydia pushed herself away and smoothed her clothes, intentionally not looking at the two women behind her. She nodded.

"Yes, I'm fine, sorry, Sheriff. I should have looked where I was going."

Angus let her go.

"You don't look fine. Come on, I'll help you to your house."

"No! I'm fine!" she exploded, wiping her tears with trembling hands.

But the sheriff's face told her he didn't believe a word she said. For a second she thought of telling him everything, but when she couldn't find the courage to do so, she turned toward her house and hurried away, disappearing behind the door before anyone could stop her.

Inside, she leaned against the door, shutting out the danger that threatened to suck her into a world of evil. Esther's words echoed in her mind. *Lies! They were all lies!* Her Rachel couldn't do what they were accusing her of. Never!

Panic coursed through her body as she realized Esther could simply push her way in. She grabbed the nearby sofa. It was heavy, but she managed to drag it across the timber floor and wedge it up against the door. No sooner had she locked the world out when she heard a knock on the door.

ANGUS HAD SEEN Esther Yoder and the other woman peering from behind the row of houses. When they saw that he had spotted them, they turned around and hurried away, raising more suspicion in his head. He'd seen the fear in Lydia Beiler's eyes. She was scared of them. Why? More importantly, why were they chasing her?

He turned back toward the Beiler home. If what James had told him was true, both Esther and Lydia knew more than they were telling him. And if they were harboring a secret, it was possible that one of them was the killer or knew who the killer was. Yet, it didn't explain Rachel's sudden disappearance. Unless Esther knew and Lydia found out. Either way, he needed answers.

His knuckles rapped on Lydia's door. When she still didn't answer the door after knocking a second time, he called out to her.

"Mrs. Beiler, it's me, Sheriff Reid. I know you're inside. We need to talk."

He waited and heard what sounded like a heavy object being dragged across the floor. Moments later the latch on the door sounded before Lydia's face appeared in the small opening of the door.

"I told you, I'm fine, Sheriff," she said gently.

"Then you won't mind me coming in to ask you about something."

"My husband isn't here."

"I am aware, Mrs. Beiler. It's you I'd like to speak with, please."

Lydia hesitated, her eyes looking past him to where Esther and Louise had stood watching her earlier.

"They've gone," Angus announced. "Can I come in now, please?"

She stepped aside and let him in, quickly shutting the door behind him.

When she turned around she couldn't bring herself to make eye contact and quickly looked away.

"I know they were chasing you. Care to tell me why?"

Lydia shook her head, her fingers playing nervously with the fabric of her dress.

"I can't help you if you don't tell me, Mrs. Beiler. Did they kill Dr. Fisher and Jonathan Lapp? Do they know where Rachel is? Did you find out and now they're trying to stop you from talking?"

"It's not like that. You won't understand," she eventually said.

"Fine, then let me ask you this. Why was Rachel seeing Dr. Fisher?"

Lydia's eyes stretched wide as they met with his penetrating gaze.

"She didn't do it, Sheriff. My Rachel didn't kill them. She couldn't do such a despicable thing."

Lydia dropped down into the chair and buried her face in her hands as she started to sob all over again. When she looked up, she had a tormented look in her eyes.

"He was an evil man, the devil himself, but she didn't kill him. You have to believe me. My Rachel isn't capable of such evil."

"She was the last one to see him alive, Mrs. Beiler. Not to mention the shoe prints that were left behind in the snow behind Mr. Lapp's barn. Why would she run if she wasn't guilty?"

Angus knew he had pushed too far but all bets were off. Time wasn't on his side. When she looked up her eyes were cold, her face stern as she spoke.

"I don't care what you or anyone else thinks, Sheriff Reid, I'm telling you, my daughter did not kill either of those men. She ran because she had no other option to save herself from the misery she knew would befall her if she stayed here."

"I want to believe you, honestly I do, but if Rachel didn't then who did?" Angus softened his tone as he continued. "Do you know who the murderer is, Mrs. Beiler?"

When she just stared at him and didn't answer he

asked again, his instincts telling him she was hiding something.

"If you know something you should tell me before the killer goes after Rachel."

His statement brought her to attention and she jumped up, her resolve in protecting her daughter evident in the way her spine had stiffened.

"I told them I won't have any part in it. Just like I know Rachel didn't do the evil things they're claiming she did."

"Who? What do they want you to do, Mrs. Beiler?"

Lydia was pacing the small room, her arms crossed over her chest as if she was giving herself a hug.

"You're talking about Esther and the other woman, aren't you? What do they want you to do? Tell me."

"They're saying Rachel killed them. That she was on some sort of rampage to kill all the other men. But she's not a murderer. My Rachel isn't a murderer."

Lydia's crying was out of control, making her gasp in between sobs and Angus walked over to where she stood in the corner of the room.

"What men, Mrs. Beiler?" His voice was urgent.

"The others who are like Dr. Fisher and Brother Lapp, who take advantage of our innocence." She sobbed harder, hiding her face in the corner.

"Please go. I've said too much already. Please, just leave."

Angus knew he was teetering on the edge of her patience, but this was his only chance to get to the truth.

"Do you know where Rachel is, Mrs. Beiler? Are you and the other women hiding her?"

Lydia whipped around, her eyes filled with rage.

"My daughter is a victim, Sheriff, not a murderer. Just like me and dozens of other women before her. Dr. Fisher and Brother Lapp got exactly what they deserved but it wasn't at my daughter's hands. She's not the only one who has enough reason to want them dead. Now please, leave my house!"

Lydia spat the words at Angus then ran into the other room and slammed the door shut behind her.

CHAPTER THIRTY-TWO

The announcement came over the two-way radio as soon as Angus stepped outside the Beilers' house. The news wasn't good and he unclipped the radio from his belt and held it closer to his ear. They were calling off the search.

Wasting no time he responded, his eyes taking in the gray clouds that foretold of another cold night.

"You can't call off the search. The girl won't survive another night out in this weather," Angus objected.

"I don't have a choice, Sheriff. The men and the dogs are tired; they need to rest. As it is, I've been rotating them. I simply don't have enough manpower to search these woods. Their safety comes first, I'm sorry. We'll pick the search up again at dawn."

When they ended the call Angus felt as if he would explode with frustration. He was so close to a break in the case, he could sense it. He looked back at the Beilers' house. He would have to break the news to the girl's mother and she wouldn't take it well. On the other hand, perhaps it would be exactly the motivation he needed to get her to talk, he thought.

He was about to knock on Lydia's door again when his cellphone rang. It was Murphy.

"Perfect timing, Murphy. I could do with hearing your voice right now," he said, desperate for some encouragement.

"Sounds like you need a shoulder to cry on, Angus. This case has you stumped, doesn't it?"

"That, Murphy, is the understatement of the year. These people are tighter than a hangman's knot, especially the women."

"The women? How so?"

"It appears our victims weren't exactly innocent. They had enemies, more than one, by the sounds of it and it's not pretty. Our victims were sexually assaulting these young girls and women, using their position as men to their advantage."

"Well, that's definitely enough motive to want to murder someone in cold blood."

"Precisely. So I guess your Amazonian frog isn't the culprit after all."

"Actually, you're wrong. That's why I'm calling - to let you know that I managed to get ahold of the composition formula and it's an exact match to the toxin I found in both victims' blood."

"Really? A frog? You're sure?"

"I've never been more certain of anything in my entire career, Angus. In fact, I can also confirm that it wasn't injected. It was applied topically, under their chins near the beard line. I missed it at first, with their beards and all covering it up, but I spotted it the moment I shaved away a small patch of hair. Identical patches, no bigger than the tip of my finger. Even a small amount is lethal enough to kill ten people. It's fascinating."

Angus grew silent as his mind worked through the information.

"I know what you're thinking," Murphy cut into his thoughts. "You're wondering how an exotic amphibian wound up here in the States. It was the very question I asked the herpetologist and, according to him, this particular venom has a lifespan of two years and can easily be stored in a vial. So, if you ask me, you're looking for someone who visited the Amazon rainforest within the last two years."

"Great, it should be a piece of cake then," Angus said with sarcasm, regretting it the moment he said it. "Sorry," he apologized, rubbing his brow. "I'm tired. This case is full of surprises. You did great work, Murph, thank you. I'll get Tammy to see what she can dig up."

"You've got this, Angus. I know the rainforest is a booming tourist destination which makes it hard to track down anyone who made a trip there but if anyone can catch our killer, it's you."

"Let's hope you're right. Word's gotten out, the pieces of this puzzle don't make sense, and I'm running out of time. Not to mention that the girl is still missing."

"I'll let you go then before it gets too dark for you to continue the search. And Angus, don't lose faith. You've got this."

After they hung up Angus made a call to Tammy instructing her to call the local airlines and travel consultants in the hope that it might yield a successful lead. When they finished, he knocked on Lydia's door.

"I have nothing more to say, Sheriff," Lydia shouted from the other side of the closed door.

"It's about Rachel," Angus answered.

Lydia yanked open the door, her face expecting good news.

"Where is she? Is she okay?"

"I'm afraid we haven't found her yet, Mrs. Beiler. The search party had to cease the search for now. The team needs to rest. But I assure you, they'll pick up the search first thing tomorrow morning."

Terror swept over her face before fresh tears filled her eyes.

"I've not given up yet. I'm going to take a few of my deputies and head out into the woods myself. I just needed to let you know."

He turned around to walk away when she spoke softly.

"The women are behind this; I just know it."

Angus turned to face her, hoping she would finally share what she had been hiding.

"Which women, Mrs. Beiler? What aren't you telling me?"

Her eyes scanned the area outside her house.

"Esther Yoder and the others, they're sabotaging your investigation. They said if they help whoever is responsible for stopping the men, we all win."

Angus' brows furrowed in concern.

"The bishop's wife? Was she a victim of the men's abuse as well?"

Lydia nodded.

"Most of us were at some point but hatred isn't what's fueling her actions. It's guilt. She blames herself for her daughter's death, not helping Joanna back when she told the bishop what some of his elders were doing. She knew the truth but chose to side with her husband, because that's what we're taught to do. Bishop Yoder refused to believe his daughter or his wife. Caleb tried to tell him too, but they chased him away, said he was causing dissension within the community and excommunicated him. Joanna, their daughter, received a shunning. But then one day she ran off into the forest. A week later, they found her clothes, ripped to shreds and covered in blood. There was blood everywhere in the spot where she was eaten alive by a black bear. It was a horrific tragedy and Esther was never the same again."

As he listened, the tiredness forgotten, Angus gained greater understanding of how the community operated.

"You need to find my Rachel. I won't be able to live with myself if she too is mauled to death by a bear. She's innocent." Her voice trailed into a gentle sob.

"I'll do everything in my power to find her, Mrs. Beiler. I give you my word."

When she shut the door, leaving Angus stunned on her doorstep, fresh adrenaline flooded his veins. He spun around, grabbing two deputies who had come back with the search party.

"We're going back in, fellas. Freshen up, grab fresh Maglites, and meet me behind the barn where Mr. Lapp was found. And hurry, we don't have much time."

Leaving the men, Angus ran to Bishop Yoder's house. He knocked twice then burst in without waiting for anyone to answer the door.

CHAPTER THIRTY-THREE

Angus exploded into the bishop's house, urgency causing him to toss all etiquette aside.

"What do you think you're doing bursting into my house like this?" Bishop Yoder demanded when Angus found him eating a sandwich at his kitchen table.

"Pardon my intrusion, Bishop, but I'm looking for your wife. It's urgent."

The bishop shot to his feet.

"Why, what's happened?" he asked as white breadcrumbs tumbled from his mouth and stuck to his beard.

"Hopefully, nothing yet so please, where is your wife?"

"She's not here. What do you mean 'nothing yet'? What exactly are you saying, Sheriff Reid?"

Angus walked to the other room and peered inside in search of Esther but the room was empty.

"I need to stop your wife before she does anything stupid."

"Stop my wife? From doing what?"

"From having someone else end up dead. Now, please, where is she?"

"You've lost your mind! My wife has nothing to do with whatever this is. Must I remind you that you are a guest—?"

"She's obstructing my investigation, Bishop. Your wife and the other women have been helping the murderer and that's breaking the law. I can arrest them for it, not to mention charge them with aiding and abetting a murderer. So, please, tell me where she is before the Beiler girl ends up like your daughter."

The bishop's face turned bright red.

"How dare you come in here and accuse my wife of such things! You have no right and you have even less right to speak of my daughter. They have nothing to do with anyone being murdered so why don't you take your men and leave my property this instant!"

Angus could have pushed back but he chose not to. Arguing with the bishop was only wasting time. Time he didn't have. He spun around and ran out the door to meet his deputies, casting a watchful eye at the sun that was already sitting low on the horizon. They set off toward the woods.

~

CALEB TRIED to lift his head off the cold forest floor, stopping when a sharp pain shot into the back of his head. He groaned, fighting off the dizzy spells that hit him. He shut his eyes tightly until it subsided enough for him to open his eyes again. Around him everything was blurry and once again he pinched his eyes closed, opening and closing them hard several times to clear his vision. His body was cold and wet, and he struggled to take control of the shivers that rippled through it. For a moment, he didn't know where he was but as his memory caught up with his surroundings, everything flooded back, and he realized that he must have passed out. For how long, he wasn't entirely certain. He squinted his eyes through the forest canopy above his head. Gray clouds sat thick above the treetops and the sun's rays were all but gone. He must have been in this spot all day, he thought when he realized that it wouldn't be long before it got dark. At first, he thought of shouting for help but then he decided against it. Someone had tried to kill him and if they were still around, there would be no chance of escaping another attack.

He flexed his neck back and spotted the arrow that was still wedged in the tree behind him. Why would anyone shoot at him, want him dead? As he pondered his situation, he wondered if this was what had happened to Rachel. He wondered if perhaps she wasn't as fast as he was and couldn't get away, if she lay dead somewhere in the forest, killed by a madman who hunted humans as if they were animals. He wondered if the forest would claim his life in the same way.

Grief overtook his spirit as the prospect of his sister being dead took root. Rachel didn't deserve to die, not like this. Unable to pull his mind away from the tragic thoughts that now plagued him, he did the only thing that was left for him to do: he bargained with God. If death came knocking on his door this day, he asked that God would take his soul instead of Rachel's. For God knew he had sinned far more than she ever did. If only God could grant him that one wish and spare his sister's life for his.

Because, if Rachel lived and he didn't, his father would finally get what his heart longed for, and he would no longer have to pretend that he didn't have a son who was alive and happy living among the English.

Caleb lingered on this last thought, his father's cursing words still echoing in his mind. Perhaps if he just lay there and accepted his fate death would come sooner. But when the leaves rustled somewhere close and fear surging through his body, he knew he loved life more than he did death. As long as he had breath in his lungs, he would fight to stay alive, with or without a father who had stopped loving him.

He pushed his body up on one elbow, craning his neck to see what had made the noise. A few yards away a deer stood alone, its big black eyes staring at him. He pushed his body further upright to have a better look but the deer startled and ran away.

"Fine friend you are," he said as he watched it disappear between the trees before his head sank back down onto the damp forest floor.

Get up! A little voice in the back of his mind told him. *No one is coming for you. It's up to you to stay alive,* the voice continued. It was true, he thought. He hadn't told anyone where he was going. He had sneaked away to go off on his own. Look what that brought him. As misery poked at his thoughts again, Rachel's innocent face flashed before his eyes. If there was even the slightest chance she was still alive, he had to take it. He had to find her.

Once more he pushed up on his elbow, paused briefly to take a look around, and tried to get up. Pain shot into his knee and forced a groan from the pit of his stomach. Amplified by the empty forest, his voice echoed between the trees throughout the quiet forest. He fell back down, dragging himself closer to the nearest tree to hide, just in case. If the hunter heard his howl and came for him, he'd have no chance of outrunning him. He waited, listened to the forest sounds, and leaned back against the tree's trunk. With wide eyes and alert ears, he searched through the shadows. Then he heard it - leaves shuffling, footsteps thumping toward him. Instantly his throat dried up as adrenaline pushed the air out of his lungs, making him pant like a tired dog in the heat of a hot summer's day. He buried his mouth behind his hand, desperate to stay hidden. Using his healthy leg, he heaved himself closer to the tree, pushing his spine against the rough bark as much as he could. Beads of sweat trickled down his temples as he shut his eyes tight, willing himself invisible.

The crunching of twigs and leaves behind him drew ever closer, telling him that it was too late. His assailant had found him.

The footsteps stopped right behind the tree, lingering in place as if to torture Caleb. He'd long since stopped breathing, pinching his eyes shut as terror overwhelmed his every sense. Suddenly the footsteps sounded beside him and even with his eyes closed, he knew something or someone was standing over him. When Caleb mustered the courage to open his eyes, deciding to face his enemy head on, what he saw instead was a fate far worse than death itself.

CHAPTER THIRTY-FOUR

Towering over his body, trapped in the snares of hatred, Samuel Beiler's dark eyes stared into Caleb's soul. His father's face was unfeeling and cold as resentment and unforgiveness clung to the deep lines around his eyes. Neither said a word, each just staring into the other's eyes for what felt like a lifetime.

When Caleb tore his eyes away from his father's stony gaze, he saw the crossbow in his father's hands, aimed in his direction. Panic ripped through his chest, his eyes darting from the loaded bow back to his father's dead eyes. Caleb tried to push himself off the slippery ground, and fight through the pain that shot relentlessly into his knee with the attempt. But as hard as he tried, he couldn't get off the ground, much less run away. He watched as his father's fingers took turns to tense over first the crossbow's grip then the bowstring, as if he was contemplating killing the son he no longer wanted, seizing the opportunity while he lay defenseless on the ground in front of him.

Caleb wanted to shout for help. But even if he was able to force a sound out of his tight throat, he knew no one would hear him. So, he stayed on the ground by his father's feet, half resting against the tree, held prisoner by the pain, his father's eyes...and the deadly weapon in his hands.

As he gazed into the eyes of the one who once vowed to love him forever, something told him that Samuel Beiler wasn't going to back off easily. Perhaps his father had every intention of pulling back on the bow and leaving him there for dead. It wasn't as if anyone would ever know anyway. If he chose to finally get rid of the son who shamed him, he would certainly get away with it.

Caleb stared into his father's eyes and swallowed hard, pushing his fear back down into the pit of his stomach where it tensed into a hard knot before courage finally found its way onto his tongue.

"Go on then, now's your chance," Caleb said, his voice strained, his eyes bravely daring.

A low grunt escaped from between his father's pursed lips as his already deep-set eyes sank even deeper below his bushy brows.

"This is your chance, Father, now, right here. Kill me. Kill the son you no longer want." Caleb's voice cracked as the words escaped from his mouth. Words he could no longer hold back. It was as if the taunting words had a will of their own, spilling from his mouth without rhyme or reason.

"You know you want to, so go ahead and do it. No one will ever know, and you'll finally be rid of me. Isn't that what you've always wanted, to get rid of your problem child, the son you wish you never had?"

Tears welled up in Caleb's eyes as his emotions got the better of him but he held his gaze. There was no taking it back now.

His father's eyes remained fixed on his, cold and unmoving, his stance frozen in place where he hovered over Caleb, bow and arrow aimed directly at his chest.

Around them, the forest grew silent as if it watched in tense anticipation. Like a sick game of chicken, neither father nor son spoke or backed away, both held prisoner by their own demons. Unable to withstand the hatred in his father's eyes a moment longer, Caleb gave in and looked away. He shifted uncomfortably, desperate to get up and out from beneath his father's domineering presence. The movement sent fresh waves of pain through his body and he stifled a moan, intent on not revealing his vulnerability. Steeling himself against his father's wrath, he looked up, expecting to see his father's angry eyes, but instead he saw them fixed upon his injured leg.

Moments later his father lowered his bow and took a step back, only then noticing the wedged arrow in the tree next to him.

"Sorry you missed," Caleb said, his voice dripping

with sarcasm as his nerves got the better of him. "I guess you should have aimed better."

His father shot him a steely look as his brows pulled into an angry frown that made Caleb immediately look away.

"It's not mine," Samuel spoke for the first time, his voice low and without emotion.

Caleb snickered.

"Yeah right, these woods are just full of fathers who hunt down their prodigal children with crossbows. If it looks like a duck and quacks like a duck, it's a duck. No use in denying it so take your chance. You might never get another one again."

"It wasn't me," his father snarled, his tone loaded with anger as he responded to his son's taunting.

The intensity of his father's voice startled Caleb, snapping him out of the false bravado he wielded to conceal his inner turmoil.

"Well, someone tried to kill me and as far as I know, you're the only person on this planet who hates me enough to want to see me dead," Caleb replied.

His callous words made Samuel look away, his gaze settling on the arrow in the tree instead. A slight frown twitched on his face as if he was trying to work through a puzzle in his head.

When he looked back at Caleb, the look in his eyes had changed. Caleb had expected his father to snap at him again. Instead, there was confusion in his eyes. He yanked the arrow out of the tree. Silence fell between them as Caleb watched his father inspect the arrow, his eyes tracing the detail from the forged steel point up the wooden shaft and the feathered fletching before it settled on the nock.

Twisting it between his thick fingers, Samuel's scrutiny lingered on the fletching which was vastly more primitive than the arrow he had in his own bow. When he had seen all there was to see, he turned around and looked back toward the forest, his eyes carefully scanning between the shadows. He turned back around to face Caleb, dropping the primitive arrow to the ground before he made a sudden motion toward Caleb. Caleb flinched and ducked behind his forearm, shielding his face as if he expected his father to attack him.

Hurt flickered in Samuel's eyes and Caleb's defensive reaction caused him to back away.

"I have no intention of hurting you, Caleb. Like I said, it wasn't me who tried to kill you. If I had wanted to, I could have done that already."

He paused before he continued.

"Do you want my help or not?"

Caleb's stomach clenched as shame and guilt set in. Was he wrong to assume his father hated him so much that he wanted him dead?

CHAPTER THIRTY-FIVE

Samuel's hand reached toward Caleb's elbow and Caleb didn't resist when his father lifted his arm across the back of his neck and draped it over his shoulders. When he hoisted Caleb up on his feet, he steadied him against the tree and took a step back.

"Can you walk?" he asked with a chilly tone.

"Why are you helping me?" Caleb blurted.

"Would you rather I leave you here to die?"

"It's what you want, isn't it? You made it very clear that I was no longer your son so what could you possibly gain by helping me now?" The questions seemed to roll off his tongue far too easily.

When his father looked at him, he had a curious look in his eyes.

"See, there's your problem, Caleb. Always questioning people's intentions, scratching at everything just so it makes sense. Not everything in life makes sense, you know. Our faith doesn't make sense. You can't go around reasoning things into being. Sometimes you just have to accept things for what they are and not go poking around where you shouldn't."

Caleb knew his father was no longer referring to the present situation.

"Even when these *things* are evil, right, Father? Is that what you expected I would do? Look the other way and live with it for the rest of my life, for the sake of religion?"

A muscle twitched below his father's right eye.

"What you did, Caleb, dishonored me in front of the entire community for all to see! You had no right to bring such shame upon our family. You knew the rules. You were raised to obey the *Ordnung* and yet you chose to deliberately act out against it. You just couldn't let it be, you had to go poking the bear. All your life I made excuses for you questioning everything, chalked it up to curiosity because your mother asked me to. But when you accused the elders of such evil, challenging my authority as your father and a member of this church, you went too far. You brought division into our community and our church, Caleb. What did you expect me to do?"

"I expected you to be the father you promised you'd be. I needed you to believe me, to stand up with me, to protect the woman I loved. Instead, you chose silence over your own flesh and blood. You picked sides, just like her father did. All those sanctimonious rules and dogmatic beliefs spoken by the very men who have nothing but evil in their hearts. The same men who stand next to you in prayer every Sunday only for them to turn around afterwards to rob young girls of their innocence, as if it is their right! And you let them. You might as well have done it yourself." Caleb shook his head as he continued. "Now, you've lost both your children and still you choose to defend this community, defend *them*! That's why Rachel left, because they were doing it to her too. But you know that already, don't you. That's why she had to take matters into her own hands and fight fire with fire, because you weren't there for her either. Rachel is probably dead because of it, just like Joanna. Driven out because of shame. But I guess that will be your cross to bear into eternity, Father. My conscience is clear. I did what I believed with every ounce of my being was the right thing to do and I would do it all over again. Because I would rather die at your hand here today knowing that I tried to help than live with the guilt of turning a blind eye and letting them get away with such evil."

Caleb's words sliced the air between them. He paused to catch his breath and slow his racing heart after the confrontation.

"Are you done?" Samuel asked, his eyes cold, his voice stern.

Caught by surprise over his father's lack of retaliation, Caleb merely nodded.

"Good, because regardless of your false accusations

and misconceptions, I still have a daughter who I love very much out here somewhere, and I believe with all my heart that she is very much alive. I'd like to find her before she's stuck out here in the cold another night fending off wild animals." He paused and let his words settle in before he continued. "I can leave you here and let you crawl your way back on your own or you can let me help you. Either way, it's your decision but make it quick, time isn't on our side."

Caleb wanted desperately to refuse his father's help but knew he couldn't. His father was right. Rachel could still be alive, and she needed them.

"I'll do it for Rachel," Caleb replied.

Without another word spoken between them, Samuel came alongside Caleb and wedged himself in under Caleb's arm, hobbling across the forest floor.

A short while later, having covered very little ground, the pain in Caleb's knee got the better of him and he broke the silence.

"I have to take a break. It hurts too much."

His father's heaving chest told him he needed to rest also.

"Fine, over there," Samuel said, pushing his hairy chin toward a large log that lay across the ground a few yards away. "We can't stay long; it's going to be dark soon." They sat down on top of it, both grateful to catch their breath.

"I know the river is just over there and there's a small

bridge a little farther that way." Caleb pointed out the direction they should take.

His father grew silent before he spoke, the tone of his voice almost dejected.

"You don't remember, do you?"

"Remember what?" Caleb responded, baffled by his father's less intimidating tone.

"I used to bring you here to fish, down there by the river. We'd spend hours sitting on the bridge, talking, watching the water rush over the rocks. You were about nine."

Caleb shook his head, noticing the sadness in his father's voice.

"I don't recall us fishing together, no."

His father got to his feet, fiddling awkwardly with his crossbow he had draped over his one shoulder.

"Doesn't surprise me. You were more interested in asking questions about the English than catching our dinner."

Caleb watched as the lines in his father's face hardened once again.

"That's enough, let's go," Samuel said. "It's almost dark and the bad weather is coming."

He moved to help Caleb onto his feet again.

"I was only trying to protect the people I loved. I never meant to bring shame upon you or the family back then," Caleb heard himself say.

His words stopped Samuel and made him back away.

"I don't want to talk about it anymore. I think you've said what you needed to."

"So that's it then, is it? You're going to just go on wishing me dead for the rest of your life."

Samuel's face turned red with anger and he spoke through clenched teeth.

"What do you want from me, Caleb?"

"I want you to own up to it. Tell me you regret not speaking up for me back then, standing up against them. You threw me under the bus and left me to fight on my own, never once defending me. You did nothing to stop them from banishing me even though you knew I was telling the truth."

"I did what I thought was the right thing to do, Caleb. I can't take it back even if I wanted to. Would I do it again? Probably not, I don't know, but I'm not going to stand here wasting precious time arguing with you about the past when I should be out there looking for my daughter instead."

It was as if Samuel's words turned the small space between them into a wall of ice, one that would never melt or go away.

"I'll get back on my own and save you the trouble and your precious time," Caleb responded, his heart damaged by his father's rejection.

Leaning over, Caleb picked up a branch from the ground in front of him and used it as a cane to get up and onto his feet.

"If I had wanted you dead, I could have killed you back there. Or, worse, left you for dead under the tree," Samuel said through pursed lips as if the half-hearted attempt at a truce made any difference now.

"Perhaps you should have. You could have saved yourself a lot of time to search for your precious daughter. She is, after all, the only child you now have left."

Caleb hobbled in one spot before he started toward the river.

But he barely moved a few yards when the now familiar sound of an arrow whistled through the chilly evening air.

Caleb spun around in search of the attacker's location, only to catch sight of the arrow sticking out from his father's shoulder moments before he watched him fall in a heap to the ground.

CHAPTER THIRTY-SIX

"Father!" Caleb yelled out and dove toward him, ignoring the stabbing pain that shot up from his knee.

"Stay down!" his father murmured, as if he had reason to think Caleb could get up on his own.

Another arrow whooshed through the air and landed in the ground next to them.

"We need to find cover," Samuel said, straining against the pain in his shoulder where his hand clutched at the lodged arrow.

"Over there." Caleb pointed his eyes at a hollow in a nearby tree.

Samuel was already on his feet, his healthy arm curled around Caleb's arm to help him up.

But Caleb struggled to get upright.

"You go. I'll be all right," he told his father. "Rachel

needs you."

Samuel didn't let go and pulled on Caleb's arm without ceasing.

"I'm not leaving you behind," he said.

One final attempt and Samuel had Caleb up, supporting him with the healthy arm as they hobbled across the small clearing toward the hollow.

"Did you get a look at the archer?" Samuel asked when they reached the opening in the tree, panting as they dropped down in front of it. The opening was barely big enough for the two of them as they squeezed in.

Caleb shook his head, his face contorted with fresh bouts of pain as his father pressed in next to him.

Another arrow slammed into the tree just above their heads, the sound of it piercing the bark reverberating like a compressed spring.

"That was too close, we can't stay here," Samuel said as he ducked lower inside the hollow. The arrow lodged in his shoulder caught on the edge of the tree as he shifted and he groaned in agony.

"You go, get help, and save Rachel. I'll only slow us down with my leg like this," Caleb said as their eyes met.

"Then we both stay. I'm not leaving my son behind."

Samuel's eyes softened and his beard twitched ever so slightly at the corners of his mouth. Quickly he turned his head away and glanced sideways at the arrow in his shoulder, a welcome distraction from the awkward silence that now hung between them.

"You need to break off the arrow. Don't pull it out, just snap it at the shaft as close to my shoulder as you can," he told Caleb.

Caleb nodded and without hesitating, wrapped his hands around the wooden shaft of the arrow.

"Lower, closer to my arm, just don't move it around too much."

Caleb did as his father said, flinching as he broke the arrow mere inches from the bleeding wound.

Twigs snapped from somewhere behind the tree. Both men froze in place, each holding their breath as they anticipated the killer coming around the tree at any moment. Only, instead of the sound of another arrow breaking the deadly silence around them, a single gunshot echoed through the forest.

Surprised, they waited in silence, each too scared to move. When silence revealed nothing about what was happening around them, Samuel carefully peered out from behind the tree. In the distance hidden behind a tree, he spotted the gunman, his weapon pointing toward an empty space not far from where they were hiding.

"It's the sheriff," Samuel announced as he sank back into the hollow.

Moments later they heard Angus' voice bellow in their direction.

"Stop or I'll shoot!"

From inside the hollow of the tree, Caleb and Samuel heard the commotion as Angus chased after the archer, footsteps thumping on the forest floor. When the sound faded into one set of stomping, they knew the attacker was running away. This time Caleb poked his head around the tree, catching a glimpse of Angus as he ran off into the forest.

"He's going after the attacker," Caleb said.

Samuel was up on his feet first, bending down to help Caleb.

"Now's our chance to get away," he said. "Hurry!"

The pair had barely gained any distance when Angus came running toward them.

"Are you okay?" he asked when he met up with them.

"We'll live," Samuel said, his eyes shut where he now leaned back against the tree trunk clutching his injured arm.

"I take it he got away," Caleb asked to which Angus replied, "my deputies are still out there looking for him.

The look on Angus' face as he stared at the broken off arrow in Samuel's shoulder told Caleb something was amiss.

Almost immediately, Angus called for medical assistance over his radio.

"I can tell something is wrong. What is it?" Caleb asked.

"How long have you been walking around with the arrow in your shoulder?" Angus asked Samuel, his eyes searching his face.

Samuel shrugged one shoulder under a grimace of pain.

"How long, Mr. Beiler?" Angus pressed him, his voice urgent.

"I don't know. It happened so quickly," Samuel responded, his tone irritated. "Why does it matter anyway?"

"It's important so take a guess."

"About ten minutes, Sheriff, maybe more," Caleb interjected.

"And you?" Angus pushed his chin out toward the specks of blood across Caleb's knee.

"This morning sometime, but I think it's just a scrape. Although it burns like fire, and I can't use it much."

Angus moved around to Caleb's knee and carefully tore open the tiny hole in his jeans. There was very little blood but his knee was big and swollen and blistering white fluid had built up and covered his entire knee.

"That doesn't look good," Samuel said as he craned his neck to see.

"You're not looking too good yourself, Mr. Beiler. It'll be better if both of you sit back down. Help is on the way so let's just sit tight here for a minute, and try to keep still," Angus said.

"Keep still? You're joking, right?" Samuel said, frustrated. "There's no time to sit still and wait for help, I'm fine. You can take care of Caleb, but I need to keep going.

Rachel won't survive another night once the sun goes down."

A frown pulled across Angus' brow.

"You're not going anywhere. This is a lot more serious than you know."

"I'll be fine, it's just an arrow, not a bullet, Sheriff. I'm a farmer. Believe me, we are quite used to treating injuries without the intervention of modern medicine."

"Not this one, I'm afraid. You're going to need to trust me, Mr. Beiler. If this is what I suspect it is, the two of you are lucky to still be alive. Now please, do as I say and keep as still as you can. The less you move the better."

"What's going on?" Caleb asked, suspicious that Angus wasn't telling them everything.

But Angus ignored his question and was already dialing a number on his cellphone. He took a few steps away from them, staring worriedly off into the forest to make his call.

"I think we've run into a problem," Caleb and Samuel heard him say. "I have two men who both got shot by an arrow, one still has it lodged in his shoulder. How long do we have? More importantly, is there an antidote?"

The look on his father's face told Caleb that his ears didn't deceive him and that he too had heard what the sheriff said.

"Antidote? What are you talking about, Sheriff?" Caleb hurled the question at Angus when he had ended his call and turned back around to face them.

CHAPTER THIRTY-SEVEN

Angus felt uneasy as he stared into Caleb's eyes. Everything about this case made him anxious and he had no control over any of it. It was as if every door to finding a resolution slammed shut in his face, kicking him out into a pit of darkness.

"We deserve to know what's going on," Caleb pleaded.

"I know, and I'm sorry. I want nothing more than to give you all the answers you need but the truth is, we are no closer to finding Rachel than we are to finding out who killed Dr. Fisher or Mr. Lapp."

"Then why are we sitting around here waiting for better days?" Samuel asked. "We should be out there looking for Rachel, or chase after the crazy guy who just tried to kill us!"

"Neither of you are in any condition to go chasing after him through the forest. I'm only taking precautions."

"Precautions for what exactly? Out with it, Sheriff. What's going on?" Samuel urged.

Angus picked his words carefully.

"We believe that the person responsible for Dr. Fisher's and Mr. Lapp's deaths used an exotic poison to kill them."

"Okay, so what? What does that have to do with finding Rachel, with us, with this?" Samuel pushed his injured shoulder towards Angus.

Angus had his hands on his hips, inwardly arguing with himself about how much he should divulge about the case.

"I might be completely wrong right now, but like I said before, I'm not taking any chances," he started. "We have reason to believe that the specific type of poison in question is one that is used by the native Amazonian people for when they go hunting. It's highly toxic and takes effect quickly, killing its target on contact."

"We're not exactly standing in the rainforest here, Sheriff," Caleb remarked.

"The Amazonian people apply the poison to the tips of their arrows." His eyes lingered on the arrow in Samuel's shoulder.

"Are you saying we're going to die?" Caleb asked looking concerned.

"I'm praying you don't, Caleb. Dr. Delaney is fairly certain you would have died by now if you had come into contact with the same poison that killed Dr. Fisher and Mr. Lapp."

Samuel pushed himself up against the nearby tree, his eyes stormy from under his bushy brows.

"You are insane, Sheriff," he said. "This isn't the first time I've been in these woods, you know, and I can tell you with absolute certainty that there are no Amazonian natives wandering around in the forest shooting poisonous arrows at people. Now, you can wait here all you want until your English doctors get here to help my son, but I am going to find my daughter before it's too late."

He turned and started walking off into the forest, clutching his arm while he searched between the shadows.

"It's not safe out here, Mr. Beiler!" Angus yelled after him.

Samuel turned and scoffed.

"I'm the one standing here with an arrow through my shoulder. Don't you think I know that, Sheriff? My daughter needs me, and I will not stand back like the coward I once was and do nothing. Not this time."

His eyes met Caleb's before he turned around and continued walking.

"What if the killer is your daughter, Mr. Beiler? Have you stopped to think about that?" Angus continued, his insides roiling with angst.

His question brought Samuel to a halt where he paused for a brief moment then turned and rushed toward Angus, his face as dark as the dusk shadows around them.

"Are you accusing my daughter of murder, Sheriff Reid? Tell me I didn't just hear you say that my child is a cold-blooded killer." He pushed his bearded face closer to Angus'.

"I'm not accusing anyone of murder yet, but I cannot deny the facts of this case. Rachel was the last one to see the doctor alive. I also have reason to believe that a woman made the footprints that were left behind in the snow behind Mr. Lapp's barn, and the person I just chased off into the forest could easily have been her for all we know. So, you tell me, Mr. Beiler, is there any reason your daughter might have wanted those men dead?"

Samuel's face was red with anger.

"She's my daughter, my flesh and blood. Even if she did have a good enough reason to want to see those men punished for their sins, why would she hunt me down, her own father? You're wrong, Sheriff. Rachel has a lot to be angry about, but I assure you she's not the one you are looking for."

Angus stared down into Samuel Beiler's eyes. They were the eyes of a father desperate to find and defend his daughter, but more than that, they were hiding a secret only Samuel knew.

"You know something, don't you, Mr. Beiler?"

Samuel turned his face and walked away, stopping in an open clearing between the trees.

"Tell him, Father, for Rachel's sake," Caleb pleaded.

But even with the short distance between them, he

could see his father's lips press together in silence under his thick beard.

"Dr. Fisher sexually assaulted my sister," Caleb blurted out. "That's what he did, cloaked it under his so-called medical treatments. As for Mr. Lapp, he and several others have been acting out their perverse pleasures for years, using their religious position over women to keep them quiet."

Caleb stopped to observe his father's face, fearing he was treading the same thin line he crossed all those years ago when he made this very accusation to the bishop. But to his surprise, his father turned to face him, his eyes revealing sadness instead of wrath.

"I know," Angus replied with dejected tone.

"You know? How?" Samuel said as he spun around to face Angus.

"Your wife told me. It seems she once fell victim to the same fate."

Hurt sat shallow in Samuel's eyes as he took in the words Angus spoke. It was as if all life drained from Samuel's face in one foul sweep of the tongue.

"I'm sorry, I just assumed you knew," Angus said as he watched Samuel walk off toward the river.

But then Samuel stopped, his eyes now fixed to his son's face.

"I did know but I buried my head in the sand, turned my back on it, on them.

Samuel's voice was thick with sorrow where he stood

alone between the trees several yards away from them. Clutching his injured arm, his chin up toward the gray skies, he spoke out loud as if he was asking God Himself.

"How could I let this happen to my wife and daughter? I was supposed to protect my family, instead allowed this secret to tear our family apart. It's my fault. I should have stood up for the truth and the integrity of my wife, my daughter. I failed them. I failed my son, and I failed God."

And as Angus and Caleb watched the agonizing heartbreak of a broken man play out in front of them, a twig snapped next to Samuel.

The attacker jumped out from behind a nearby tree and wedged a large hunting knife against Samuel's throat.

CHAPTER THIRTY-EIGHT

Angus pulled his gun and aimed it directly at the attacker who now stood behind Samuel, his arms curled around Samuel's shoulders, the blade pushing up against his neck. From behind the dirty rags that draped around his head covering everything except his eyes, he stared fiercely at Angus.

Angus held his position, his gun pointed firmly toward the assailant. Samuel groaned as the man tightened his grip around his shoulders and pulled his head back toward the folds of the filthy cloth that concealed his identity.

"Let him go," Angus said, his eyes locked to the wild man's gaze.

His warning did nothing but antagonize the attacker even more, evident by the way he pulled back harder on Samuel's body. Angus didn't ease up either, fully convinced the man would back off.

Except he didn't. Nor did he flinch. His body showed no fear. He remained sturdy and planted firmly behind Samuel as if he'd rehearsed the scene a thousand times. Eager to find his weakness, Angus studied the man's clothing. His dark green trousers were made from thick corduroy that frayed at the hems as age had worn them down. On his upper body he wore an oversized padded men's flannel bomber jacket, the once bright yellow checkered blocks dulled by years of dirt. A bow draped loosely over one shoulder, flanked by the strap of a cross-body leather satchel that rested on his hip. Covering his hands were dirt-stained fingerless knitted gloves, the once beige color barely recognizable as they too had seen better days. When Angus directed his attention to the man's hands, he noticed that the one across Samuel's chest was missing several digits. One of his fingers was entirely missing; three were short stumps of different lengths. They looked scrawny, like they belonged to someone who was underfed. When the attacker saw that Angus was staring at his deformed hand he growled like an ape man, uttering sounds instead of words, tugging and shuffling Samuel's body as if to force Angus to look elsewhere.

"Just let him go, okay. No one wants to get hurt here today," Angus attempted to defuse the situation.

But still, the attacker didn't budge.

From where Caleb sat against the tree, he yelled at the madman.

"Let my father go! He's old, take me and finish the job you started this morning."

Angus wanted to tell Caleb to be quiet but when he spotted the curious look in the attacker's eyes where he now looked full into Caleb's face, something told him to let it play out. A tense minute went by, each armed man holding his stance, waiting for his opponent to back down.

"Why are you doing this? What do you want with us?" Caleb asked, hoping to negotiate the dire situation in their favor.

But his question did the opposite and he watched in agony as the man yanked the knife away from his father's throat and flipped it into a stabbing position. His fingers tightened over the handle, gripping it with vigor where he now pointed the blade at Samuel's heart.

Caleb gasped in horror.

Angus warned at the same time.

"That would be a wrong move on your part. If you stab him, you will have no time to dodge the bullet from my gun, and from experience I can assure you, you will have as much chance of surviving a bullet in the chest as he would getting stabbed by your knife. Trust me, it's not worth it."

Angus paused, assessed the effect of his warning as he waited for the man to react.

When he didn't, the knife in his hand still hovering dangerously close to Samuel's chest, Angus repeated Caleb's question.

"What do you want with him? Why were you trying to kill them? We can talk about this, without our weapons. I can help you."

Once again, the untamed man growled, this time following the wild grunt with a higher pitched scream as if he was frustrated with something. Realizing the voice wasn't male, Angus studied his jacket more closely. It was the same person he had chased into the woods earlier.

"Put the knife down and let's talk, Rachel," he ventured, but noticed the wrinkle between her eyes as her brows pulled closer.

The knife was back up against Samuel's throat.

"Rachel? Is it you?" Samuel asked with a gentle voice. "I'm sorry I didn't believe you. I'm sorry I wasn't there for you. Please, put the knife down so we can talk."

The woman ignored him and instead, shuffled them in unison toward Caleb, shielding her body with Samuel's. When she stopped in front of Caleb, she looked down at his face.

Silent, sitting against the tree, Caleb met her gaze.

"I see you still haven't grown a spine," she spoke for the first time, her words muffled by the draped cloth over her face.

"That hurts, Rachel, considering we haven't seen each other in years," Caleb said, desperate to help defuse the situation.

She didn't answer.

Angus slowly rotated to face them, carefully taking a few steps toward them.

"Stay there!" she yelled when she spotted his movements. "Go over there or I'll slit his throat. Don't think I won't do it! And drop your gun!" She tightened her grip on the knife at Samuel's neck.

Something in her voice told Angus she wasn't making idle threats, and he tossed his gun to one side.

"Fine, just put the knife away," he said, his palms now out toward her.

"I'll decide what happens here, not you. No man will ever tell me what to do again, you hear me?" Her voice was near hysterical.

"Fine, I get it, I don't like to be told what to do either," Angus said.

She scoffed.

"You don't get it, none of you will ever get it. You're men! Filthy, slimy, disgusting men who think you own us. Well, you don't!"

Angus didn't drop his guard; his eyes remained fixed on hers.

"Is that why you killed Dr. Fisher and Jonathan Lapp?" Angus asked, ready to lunge into action if she made good on her threats.

"They got what they deserved."

Unable to hold back, Caleb responded in surprise.

"It was you, you killed them? How could you do that, Rachel?"

"I am not RACHEL!" she yelled, angered by his assumption.

"Then who are you and why do you want us dead?" Caleb pushed back.

"Best to leave the questions to the sheriff, Caleb," Samuel strained to speak the caution sideways toward Caleb. She pushed the knife down harder into the soft folds of his neck. He sucked in through his teeth when the blade cut into his flesh leaving blood trickling onto his collar.

"Easy now," Angus said when he saw the tense look in her eyes. "No one needs to get hurt."

But her gaze was fixed to Caleb's face, searching his eyes for answers he did not know the questions to.

"Rachel, put down the knife," Caleb responded. "I'm sorry I left you behind. I should have taken you with me. If I knew..." He dropped his head to his chest. "Please, let's not make things worse than they already are."

"I told you already! I'm not Rachel." Her jaw was clenched as she spat the words at him.

"Then who are you? Tell us," implored Angus.

"Clearly you know who we are," Caleb said. "So why don't you show your face?"

His daring request made her fidgety and she looked away.

"No," her answer came abruptly. "Now stop talking or I'll end him right here. God knows he deserves to die just like they did."

"No one deserves to die. Taking the law into your own hands isn't the way to go about this," Angus said.

She scoffed.

"Is that so? Tell me, Officer, which man carries the consequence of the sin? The one who sharpens the blade of the knife or the one who uses it to slit a man's throat."

CHAPTER THIRTY-NINE

The woman's question lingered in the tense silence as they stood in the middle of the forest.

"Choosing what you do with that knife in your hand is entirely up to you," Angus replied. "No one is telling you what to do but if you choose to use it to hurt an innocent man, you need to be prepared for the consequences."

Angus had barely finished his sentence when she moved the knife into her other hand and yanked down on the rag that covered her face, unwrapping it until her entire face was exposed.

Caleb drew in a sharp breath as the horrific motive for hiding her face revealed itself.

"Did they stop to think about the consequences of their actions before they did this to me? Because I certainly had no say in this. They had no right to claim my body as their own, to do with it as they pleased. No one believed me, not even you, Caleb! Oh sure, you *tried*, but we both know all you did was have one spineless conversation with my father. And surprise, surprise, not even my own father did anything to make those men pay for what they did to me and to the countless other women in our community. They never faced any consequences, ever, and no one stopped them. Each day that the sun rises they're at it again, getting away with it over and over again. So, I did what I needed to do to stop it from continuing, from hurting people like Rachel. I did what no one else had the courage to do. I banished them to hell where they belong!"

Her voice trailed off as her shoulders sagged and deep sorrow overcame her. It was blatant to all three men listening to her confession that the deep sadness had been lying dormant and festering for years. Tears streamed over the deep scars on her face, the poorly healed rippled remnants of something that had once carved into the flesh on her face and neck leaving nothing but pain and shame in its wake.

"Yes, take a good look at what all of you men did to me! I was left for dead, tossed out with the garbage like my life was worth nothing. Left and forgotten in the wild to be mauled by a bear, just like you tried to do with Rachel. Well, I wasn't going to let the same happen to her, just as I won't let you get away with turning a blind eye to the despicable acts of those evil men."

Angus watched as she pulled back on Samuel's body,

the knife now positioned just below his left ear as she readied herself to send him to an early death.

"Don't do it, Joanna!" Caleb yelled out as he pieced together her identity, causing her to look directly at him.

Fresh tears filled her eyes as they stared at each other.

"I did everything I could to help you, I promise I did. I did more than just talk to your father; I threatened them, the elders, the entire community. I told them to put an end to it or I would. He forbade me to see you and put me in shunning. I tried to get a message to you, but your father intercepted it and told me you had run away and that they had found your bloody clothes in the forest. They said a bear killed you. I don't know why I believed them, but I did. I was young, naive and I'm sorry. They kicked me out, chased me away like I was a stray dog. I failed you. I failed us." Caleb sobbed, his shoulders bent forward and shaking under the weight of his broken heart.

"You weren't the one who did wrong, Caleb," Samuel spoke, his eyes filled with regret as he looked at Caleb. "You were right. You're my son, my only son, and I should have believed you, stood by you, done more to stop this. I should have protected Rachel. Joanna's right. I'm as much to blame as those men - for you leaving, for Rachel having to suffer, for keeping this despicable secret, for not doing anything to stop it. But I can't take it back. All I can ask is that you forgive me, both of you. If I could do it all over again, I'd do it differently. My cross is heavy, too heavy to carry by myself. The guilt is crushing me. If it means this is my punishment for looking the other way then I'll take it. As God is my witness. Just please, don't let my children suffer. Tell the sheriff where Rachel is before you kill me."

Joanna sniffed then dried her tears against her shoulder, her scarred face revealing her inner turmoil.

"Let him go, Joanna, and tell us where Rachel is, please?" Caleb begged.

But the look in Joanna's eyes told Angus she had no intention of giving in to Caleb's plea.

"How did you get ahold of the poison, Joanna?" Angus diverted her attention, knowing that help was imminent. All he needed to do was buy more time until it got there.

His question surprised her, threw her off her game just like Angus had hoped it would.

"So, you figured it out then. I'm impressed. Not many people know it even exists. A tiny golden creature with the power to kill prey a thousand times its size, hidden away in the jungle. Underestimated, if you ask me." The double meaning was evident in her words.

"Like you," Angus continued.

"Yes, like me! But I showed them, didn't I? I taught them a lesson they will never forget. They close us off from the world, from all it has to offer. At first, I thought it was to protect us; now I know it was to keep us from learning the truth. When I killed that bear with my bare hands, smashing his head in with the rock, I knew I was strong enough to stop the wicked ways of those men too. It didn't matter that the bear clawed my face and ripped my fingers off. I knew I had survived for a reason. All I had to do was find a way to make them pay for what they did. You won't believe what you can learn on the internet. Taking that trip to the zoo was the most freeing thing I've ever done." She smiled. "And when they needed an extra hand during the summer, I jumped at the opportunity. Who knew stealing the venom of a little golden frog would be that easy?"

"Your mission was a success so why not let Samuel go? The poison is most likely working its way through his body as we speak."

"I'm not the ruthless killer you think I am. I have no intention of wasting my poison on Samuel. He's just collateral damage."

"Let him go, Joanna. He's innocent," Caleb pleaded once more.

Her eyes pierced Caleb's when she turned to face him.

"Why are you protecting him after all he's done to you, Caleb? He betrayed you, discarded and disowned you just like my father did to me."

Caleb smiled, peace written all over his face.

"Because I believe in second chances, Joanna, in forgiving others, in letting go of the things that weighed me down. I forgave my father a long time ago, your father too, and placed all my hurt and anger at the foot of the cross, for God to work out according to His purpose. You should do the same, Joanna. *That* will be the most freeing thing you'll ever do. I guarantee it."

Angus watched as Caleb's words washed over Joanna. The truth of his words quieted her soul until she loosened her grip on Samuel and let the knife fall onto the ground by their feet along with her burdens.

All the frustration and confusion Angus had about this case cleared away, and he knew the reason why the case had him running around in circles.

God needed time to set in motion all the parts that brought together this exact moment, so that both Samuel and Joanna could find their way to redemption.

Joanna dropped to her knees next to Caleb, her head resting on his shoulder not able to stand under the years of festering hatred, as the rescue team came rushing toward them.

CHAPTER FORTY

Angus fastened the handcuffs around Joanna's wrists and turned her around to face him.

"I will make sure you get the best defense attorney in my county, Joanna, and I'll do my utmost to see that the judge takes the mitigating circumstances under consideration. No one should have endured what you did. I give you my word that I will conduct a thorough investigation and bring to justice every single man in the community who has ever wronged a woman in this way. But this is your time to make things right. Tell us where Rachel is. Did you take her? Do you know where she is, Joanna?"

Fresh tears spilled from Joanna's eyes and she nodded.

"I saved her. She was out there in the cold, washed up on the banks of the river when I found her. Her head was covered in blood, and she was barely breathing. She had a letter in her hand, addressed to Caleb. She had written to him about Dr. Fisher and what he had done to her. But I knew that already, so I left the letter in the river. I had been watching him for months, and saw her leave his office, her head bowed in shame. I knew the signs. That's why he had to die first. I couldn't let him get away with it any longer. All it took was one swift dab of a poisonous paintbrush under his chin. Seducing an evil man is easier than you might think." Joanna grew quiet.

"Where is she now, Joanna? Where's Rachel?" Angus pushed.

"I picked her up and carried her to my cabin. It's about a fifteen minute walk that way until you get to the tree with the split trunk. It's on the other side of the ridge. I did what I could for her, bound her head up to stop the bleeding, but she never woke up."

Angus' heart caught in his throat as he waited for her to finish.

"She needs to be in hospital. I did what I could, but she needs proper doctors."

"She's still alive?" Angus urged.

Joanna nodded.

Angus handed Joanna over to one of his deputies and watched him lead her away. He flagged down two rescue personnel and bolted toward the cabin. As they crested the ridge, Angus spotted the small rustic cabin nestled between the trees. Wasting not a single moment, they slid down the side of the hill and found Rachel unconscious on a small cot inside the cozy cabin, her head wrapped in a homemade bandage, just like Joanna had said.

"Rachel, can you hear me?" Angus tried, but she didn't respond and he stood aside and let the rescue team take charge.

"She'll be all right, Sheriff," one of them said after he checked her vitals and the wound on her head as he made the necessary preparations to get her to hospital.

When they carried her to a nearby clearing where a medevac helicopter would soon pick them up, Angus looked around the rest of the cabin. The single room had nothing but a cot, a humble make-shift kitchen, and a small bookshelf, all constructed out of branches no doubt collected from the forest. Much to his surprise there was no sign of any bright yellow amphibians anywhere and he turned his attention to the small collection of books on the shelf next to him. There were a few threadbare Agatha Christie novels, an encyclopedia, and a couple of magazines. Nothing out of the ordinary. As he crouched down to have a better look, his eyes caught sight of a small box that lay half concealed on the floor behind a chipped porcelain jug. He took off the top half of the box and found two small antique medicine bottles half filled with clear liquid inside. It had to be the extracted toxin used to murder Dr. Fisher and Jonathan Lapp.

His heart sank as he stared down at the glass bottles.

Although Joanna had confessed to both murders, part of him had hoped that he wouldn't find any evidence to corroborate her confession. She had endured much, too much, had been driven to kill because no one wanted to help her. An image of her disfigured face popped into his head and he knew that it was going to be one of those cases that would never leave him.

As he swallowed down the bitter taste of disdain that lay in the back of his throat, he quietly vowed to make good on his promise to her and bring justice to those men who had gotten away with such wickedness for far too long.

LATER THAT EVENING, Angus closed the case file and shut the lid of his laptop. He stared into the flickering flames of his fireplace. Thrilled as he was with the outcome of the case, he couldn't tear his mind away from it.

Deep in thought and prayer, a knock at his door interrupted his musings and he got up to answer it.

"I thought you might need a distraction," Murphy said when he answered the door.

"Dr. Delaney, you know me far too well."

She blushed and looked down at the envelope in her hand.

"Actually, I came to bring you this. It's the results of

your ancestry test. I thought you might like to focus on something else."

Angus took the envelope from her hand as he ushered her inside.

"Right, I'd forgotten all about it. Thanks for bringing it over."

"This case had your head that busy?"

He nodded, signaling her to sit down.

"I just cannot get over the fact that a young girl like Joanna had to take justice into her own hands to get help. It just isn't fair. There should have been a way for them to report these things without going against the *Ordnung*."

"It's how they do things in the Amish communities, though, Angus. It's not your fault, you know. You saved that community by not giving up, gave those women the courage to speak up and expose the two elders who groomed those girls for Dr. Fisher. And Joanna, she's getting the help she needs. That prison therapy program is one of the best and it's all thanks to you. You did your job, Angus."

"Then why do I feel like I've somehow failed? None of this would have happened if they had had the means to get help before it resulted in such drastic measures."

"Perhaps. Although, sometimes you have to let God do the work He needs to do, His way. Like that report in your hands, for example." She smiled sweetly. "Are you going to open it or not?"

Angus paused, his eyes lingering on the manila envelope.

"Whatever it says, Angus, I'm here for you."

He gave Murphy a brave smile and tore open the seal and slid the single sheet of paper from the envelope. When he had finished reading it, he handed it to Murphy who did the same.

"At least now I know, right?" he said, as he watched her eyes linger on the line that confirmed that Logan Reid was his brother, the big bold letters next to it reading: deceased.

FROM THE OTHER side of the dinner table, Caleb opened his eyes halfway through the dinner prayer. Rachel sat opposite him. Even with the bandage still covering the nasty gash on her head from the rocks in the river, she looked like an angel. With the innocence of a child, she sat praying, her palms together under her chin, her eyes closed as her lips curled into a slight smile. Next to her, his mother oozed peace also, her soft smile telling him that she had let go of all her burdens. His gaze lingered on his father's face. He was praying; his hands clasped in front of his chest, his lips moving under his beard. The lines on his face had softened since he had first seen him just a few days ago, the anger gone. The Potter had shaped them all, changing their hearts to accept each other's differences. It no longer mattered that they did things differently or had certain ceremonial habits that set them apart in their walk with Christ. Sinner or saint they were one family.

And as Caleb quietly savored being welcome in his family's home again, he learned the lesson God had set before him. At the foot of the cross, there was level ground and as long as they looked to their Savior, His grace would always take them home.

"Come to Me, all who are weary and heavily burdened [*by religious rituals that provide no peace*], *and I will give you rest"* [*refreshing your souls with salvation*].

- Matthew 11:28 -

(AMP)

Thank you for reading Caleb's Cross. I pray that God touched you in a divine way, just like He did me while writing it.

Please help other readers find this book by leaving a review.

Just a few words or a star rating will suffice. Thanks in advance!

Sheriff Angus Reid delves into a new case in book 4, Hannah's Halo.

Sign up for exclusive sneak peeks and updates.

Newsletter.urcelia.com/signup

For a full and updated list of all Urcelia Teixeira books, please visit https://shop.urcelia.com/pages/reading-order

MORE BOOKS BY URCELIA TEIXEIRA

Angus Reid Mysteries series

Jacob's Well

Daniel's Oil

Caleb's Cross

Adam Cross series

Every Good Gift

Every Good Plan

Every Good Work

Jorja Rose trilogy

Vengeance is Mine

Shadow of Fear

Wages of Sin

Alex Hunt series

The Papua Incident (FREE!)

The Rhapta Key

The Gilded Treason

The Alpha Strain

The Dauphin Deception

The Bari Bones

The Caiaphas Code

More books coming soon! Sign up to my newsletter to be notified of new releases, giveaways and pre-release specials.

MESSAGE FROM THE AUTHOR

All glory be to the Lord, my God who breathed every word through me onto these pages.

I have put my words in your mouth and
covered you with the shadow of My hand
Isaiah 51:16

It is my sincere prayer that you not only enjoyed the story, but drew courage, inspiration, and hope from it, just as I did while writing it. Thank you sincerely, for reading *Caleb's Cross.*

I appreciate your help in spreading the word, including telling a friend. Reviews help readers find books! Please leave a review on your favorite book site.

ABOUT THE AUTHOR

Award winning author of faith-filled Christian Suspense Thrillers that won't let you go!™

Urcelia Teixeira, writes gripping Christian mystery, thriller and suspense novels that will keep you on the edge of your seat! Firm in her Christian faith, all her books are free from profanity and unnecessary sexually suggestive scenes.

She made her writing debut in December 2017, kicking off her newly discovered author journey with her fast-paced archaeological adventure thriller novels that readers have described as 'Indiana Jones meets Lara Croft with a twist of Bourne.'

But, five novels in, and nearly eighteen months later, she had a spiritual re-awakening, and she wrote the sixth and final book in her Alex Hunt Adventure Thriller series. She now fondly refers to *The Caiaphas Code* as her redemption book. Her statement of faith. And although this series has reached multiple Amazon Bestseller lists, she took the bold step of following her true calling and switched to writing what honors her Creator: Christian Mystery and Suspense fiction.

The first book in her newly discovered genre went on to win the 2021 Illumination Awards Silver medal in the Christian Fiction category and the series reached multiple Amazon Bestseller lists!

While this success is a great honor and blessing, all glory goes to God alone who breathed every word through her!

A committed Christian for over twenty years, she now lives by the following mantra:

"I used to be a writer. Now I am a writer with a purpose!"

For more on Urcelia and her books, visit https://www.urcelia.com

To walk alongside her as she deepens her writing journey and walks with God, sign up to her Newsletter - https://newsletter.urcelia.com/signup

or

Follow her at

goodreads.com/urcelia_teixeira
facebook.com/urceliateixeira
bookbub.com/authors/urcelia-teixeira
amazon.com/author/urceliateixeira
instagram.com/urceliateixeira
pinterest.com/urcelia_teixeira

Made in the USA
Las Vegas, NV
02 March 2024